CONSUMED

A Devil Chaser's MC Romance

L Wilder

Cover by: Carrie at cheekycovers.com

Editor: Brooke Asher
www.facebook.com/pages/Brooke-Asher-Editing/517436751724676

Cover Model: Chris Childers
www.facebook.com/ChrisChildersFitness

Cover Photographer: Geof Hutton
www.facebook.com/geof.hutton

Quotes from: www.brainyquote.com
Original author sited in each.

DEDICATION

To Brooke

The Devil Chaser Romance Series wouldn't even exist without you. Thank you for encouraging me to write and helping me make my dream come true. You are, and always will be, my best friend.

A Special Thank You:

To Marci

Even when your world was surrounded in chaos, you still found time to help me with this book. I can't tell you how much your dedication has meant to me.

PROLOGUE

Revenge is the act of passion;
Vengeance is an act of justice.
Samuel Johnson

BOBBY

———◦◦◦———

I T'D BEEN TEN days… ten long, agonizing days of watching Courtney continue to fade away. Even after tons of tests and constant monitoring, the doctors couldn't tell me why she wasn't waking up. They kept telling me to give it time. Fuck, I'd given it time, but nothing had changed. The room was still so quiet. Courtney always lit up every room she entered, smiling and talking a mile a minute. There was never a dull moment when she was around. Since she'd been in the hospital, though, everything had gone silent. The only sound I could hear were the annoying beeps of all the machines they had her hooked up to.

Our VP, Goliath, had come by earlier and finally broken the news to me about her wreck. His words kept replaying over and over in my head. "*It wasn't an accident.*" Someone had actually done this on purpose. We were certain that the Black Diamonds had something to do with it, but it just didn't make any sense to me. Why would they go after her? She'd never done anything to deserve this. It had to be a direct hit against the club. If she hadn't been with me, they wouldn't have ever gone after her. I'd failed her. I hadn't kept her safe, and that thought haunted me every time I looked at her lying in that hospital bed.

I needed to get to the clubhouse to see what I could find out about the Black Diamonds. Courtney's parents usually spent their days with her, so I knew she wouldn't be alone. It cut me up inside to leave her, even if it was only for a few hours, but I needed to find out who had hurt her. I had to find something useful… anything we could use against them.

No one was at the clubhouse when I got there, so I could focus on what I needed to do. I hacked into every site in my database, and I didn't like what I found. The Black Diamonds were a small 1 Percenter's club based out of Detroit, and they were building their charter rapidly, by any means necessary. They moved into small towns across the country and used intimidation and money to gain control of the area. They were all about numbers, recruiting anyone to get their drugs on the streets and cash into the club's pockets.

When I finished my research, I went over to the meeting room for church. The Devil Chasers' president, Bishop, had called us in to discuss everything that had gone down over the past few days. Once everyone was there, I shared what I had learned about the Black

Diamonds. Bishop and Goliath told us that it would take time to forge an effective plan, and we needed to be on high alert. The longer I listened, the more impatient I became. I could feel my blood boiling through my veins as I thought about Courtney lying in that hospital. I wanted to go down to their warehouse and rip their fucking throats out for what they had done to her. I took a deep breath and tried to concentrate on what Bishop was saying.

"Crack Nut," he said as he looked over to me, "we need eyes on their warehouse. I want to know where they are making their deliveries, and when the next shipment is coming in. I want to make sure we get them where it hurts."

"I'm on it," I told him.

"Take Goliath and Renegade with you. No mistakes here. I don't want them to have any idea that we're watching them."

I nodded, knowing what he was implying. We had left too many clues behind when we'd set up our surveillance at the Red Dragon's compound, and it could have cost us.

As soon as we were dismissed from church, I went straight to the hospital. As I walked into Courtney's room, I noticed a small Christmas tree on the bedside table. Her parents had been there, but thankfully they'd already left for the day. I really wasn't in the mood to see them. Being there was hard enough without seeing her mother crying nonstop. I knew she blamed me for the accident, but she tried to keep her focus on Courtney.

Her father, on the other hand, made his feelings a bit more obvious. He constantly glared at me and never tried to conceal the disgust and anger in his eyes. I didn't blame him. I deserved it. She wouldn't have been in that hospital bed if it weren't for me.

I walked over to her bed and pulled a chair close to the side of the bed to be next to her. God, I missed her. It was the little things that got to me most. I'd always loved holding her hand, feeling the soft touch of her hand in mine. I needed to feel her… to touch her… so I took her hand and slowly rubbed my thumb across her fingers. I closed my eyes and took a deep breath to calm my nerves. Trying to break the unbearable silence, I began talking to her, praying that she might actually hear me.

"We had church today to talk about what we're going to do to the guys that hurt you. I won't let them get away with it, Court. I love you so much. I don't know if I can stand this much longer. I need you to come back to me. I need you to keep me from falling over the edge. Please, baby… come back to me." I looked up and searched her face for any signs of consciousness. Nothing.

Her beautiful voice constantly soothed and entertained me. The silence was like a knife in my heart. I needed her to say something, to keep me from losing my mind. I didn't know what else to do. We'd tried everything to wake her up. Her mother had brought in her iPod so that she could listen to her favorite music. We'd filled the room with her favorite flowers, and we were constantly talking to her and touching her like the doctors had told us to. She never even budged. Sometimes, I thought maybe she was just being stubborn.

"Court, you have to wake up. You've kept me waiting long enough. I need you, baby," I pleaded with her. I'd said it all before, but still I got no response. She just lay there with her eyes closed like she was sleeping. Her face was pale, and she'd lost weight. I hated it. I couldn't stand watching her fade away right in front of my eyes. Every time I looked at her, it fueled my need for revenge. I was consumed by my hatred.

I was so tired that I could barely keep my eyes open, so I finally gave in to my exhaustion. I closed my eyes and rested my forehead on her leg. I had almost fallen asleep when I felt her fingertips brush through my hair. I thought it was just my imagination until I felt it again. I lifted my head and saw Courtney opening her eyes.

"Court?" I whispered. "Can you say something? Let me know I'm not dreaming here, baby. Say something."

Her eyes flickered open and shut several times before she fell back to sleep. She'd never opened her eyes, so for the first time in days, I felt hope. Hope that she might find her way back to me. I sat there for hours, watching for any sign of life from her. I talked to her and rubbed her hand, praying that she would find the strength to wake up.

I don't know when exactly I fell asleep. I woke up as one of the nurses came in to check Courtney's vitals.

"She tried to open her eyes last night," I told her as I leaned forward in my chair.

"That could be a good sign, Bobby. It could mean

that she's about to wake up. It's important to keep talking to her. She needs all the stimulation she can get. Familiar sounds and touch tend to make a really big difference in helping patients find their way back."

"I was talking to her last night when it happened."

"That's good. Keep it up. Have some of her friends come by and visit with her. Every little bit helps," she explained.

"Do you think she's going to pull through this?" I asked.

"If I knew a guy like you was waiting for me, I would do everything I could to get back to you. I'm sure she feels the same way." God, I hoped she was right. It seemed like I'd been waiting for a lifetime.

Just as the nurse was leaving, Courtney's doctor came in to review her chart. He turned to me and said, "We need to do another MRI to evaluate the residual function of the brain." I hated the idea of them doing more tests on her, but I couldn't tell him no.

"Do whatever you need to do to bring her back to me," I told him feeling totally defeated.

"We'll do what we can. You keep talking to her and let me know if there is any change."

I spent the next few hours watching her and praying for some kind of sign that she would wake up. She'd move her hand, or blink her eyes, but nothing more. The doctors said something about her being in a minimally conscious state and that I needed to be patient. The wait was excruciating, but I had to hope that she would eventually find her way back.

CHAPTER 1

COURTNEY

———◦◦◦———

SOMETHING WASN'T RIGHT. I was having such a hard time waking up. There was a hand moving up and down my arm, so I knew someone was there with me. I could hear the sounds of their mumbled words, but I couldn't understand what they were saying. I had no idea why I was in such a haze. My body felt so heavy, and it was difficult to move. I tried to lift my hand, but I felt so weak. I just wanted to go back to sleep.

"That's it, baby. You gotta keep fighting. Come back to me, Court," Bobby said with such love in his voice that it tore at my heart.

I finally forced myself to open my eyes enough to see him standing there beside me. Even with my blurred vision, I could see the worry in his eyes. He had dark circles under them like he hadn't slept in days. I still couldn't understand what was going on, but I could tell by looking at him that something awful had happened.

"Court, can you talk to me? I need you to say something, baby," Bobby pleaded.

I was stuck in a fog. Everything was moving so slowly, and I couldn't clear my head. My mouth felt like it was filled with cotton, and my throat was completely dry. It had to be the worst hangover in the history of all hangovers. I felt *terrible*. I cleared my throat and was finally able to say, "Bobby…?"

He leaned over and kissed me on the lips. He brushed my hair out of my face as he reached over and hit the nurse's call button. "I can't believe it. You came back to me," he said excitedly.

"What…? What's going on?" I asked.

He kissed me again before he said, "You're in the hospital, baby. There was an accident." He continued to rub his hand gently down my arm as he spoke. I tried to think back, but I couldn't remember anything.

Before he could continue, a nurse rushed in and asked, "Is everything okay?"

"She's awake!" Bobby said as he stepped out of the nurse's way.

"Welcome back, honey. You gave us all quite a scare," she told me. She hit the call button again and told them to send the doctor to my room. "We need to run some tests, Bobby. You'll need to go out in the waiting room for a little while."

It took the doctors several hours to do all their "tests". I felt like a bug under a freaking microscope as they checked all my vitals. The doctor told me they would do more testing over the next few days, but he was confident I would make a full recovery. I was still struggling to understand how I got there in the first place, so I asked, "Why can't I remember what happened?"

"It's perfectly normal, Courtney. Things may come back to you slowly or all at once. Just give it some time. I'm sure your family can help you put the pieces together," the doctor replied.

"This all seems so strange," I told him. "I feel so lost." Physically, I was already feeling better, but I was still confused about everything that was happening.

"That's understandable. Just give it time. I'll be back later tonight to check on you, but call me if you need anything."

"Thank you, Doctor," I told him as he walked out of the room. It wasn't long before Bobby came back in.

"You doing okay?" he asked.

"I don't know. I can't even remember how I got here, Bobby."

"You crashed your car into a ravine on the way to the clubhouse ten days ago. You've been in a coma," Bobby said with concern in his voice. "You were babysitting John Warren for Lily and…."

"Oh my God! Was he with me? Is John Warren okay?!" I asked frantically. I panicked at just the thought of him being hurt. He was still so little, and even so Lily had trusted me to watch him. I wouldn't have been able to live with myself if anything had happened to him.

"He's fine, baby. Everything is fine. None of that matters now. We just need to focus on getting you better," he said calmly.

How was it possible that I'd been in a coma for so long? Just hearing him say the words out loud changed something inside me. I could see my life laid out in front of me, and I didn't like what I saw. There was so much more I wanted for myself. I felt empty. So much had been happening around me, and I'd been stuck waiting on my life to begin. I'd wasted so much time, and I couldn't ignore my feelings any longer.

The pit in my stomach grew deeper as I watched Goliath and Lily come into the room. They were followed closely behind by Renegade and Taylor. Seeing them standing there only reminded me of what I didn't have. Bobby gave my hand a quick squeeze before he walked over to greet them at the door. My heart twisted as I watched Goliath move closer to Lily and wrap his arm around her waist. The agonizing tightness in my chest grew as I glanced over to Renegade and Taylor. He stood only inches from her, claiming her in an unspoken embrace. I was being stupid. Seeing them like that shouldn't have bothered me, but it did. These men knew what they wanted, and they didn't let anything stand in their way. No obstacles, big or small, could've kept them apart. It should've been that way with Bobby, and it pissed me off that it wasn't. I was angry with him for not showing me *that* kind of love and furious with *myself* for letting it go on for so long.

As soon as Bobby finished talking to them, Lily and Taylor rushed over and hugged me tight.

"I was so excited when Bobby called to tell us you had finally decided to wake up. Courtney, you had us scared to death!" Lily told me excitedly.

"I'm still trying to wrap my head around everything

that's happened. This whole thing is so surreal. I can't believe I've actually been in a *coma*," I explained.

"It was awful seeing you like that. I kept expecting you to pop up and start telling us one of your wild stories," Taylor said with a smile.

"You know me… it won't be long before I'll be driving you all nuts again," I said, forcing a laugh.

We'd only been making small talk for a few minutes when Bobby said, "Guys… I really appreciate y'all coming by, but Courtney needs her rest."

"No! Don't go yet," I told Lily as I took hold of her hand. "I… I need to talk to Lily alone." After being with them all together, I wasn't ready to be alone with Bobby. The reality of our relationship was crashing down on me, and I wasn't ready to deal with it just yet. I needed time to sort things out.

"You need your rest," he told me firmly.

"*No*, Bobby. You're not listening to me. I need some time *alone* with Lily," I snapped.

Irritation spread across his face as he said, "I'll give you some time, but I'm not going anywhere. I'll be outside if you need me." He leaned over and kissed me on the forehead before he walked out of the room. My heart sank as I watched him go. Something inside of me had changed, and I didn't understand it. I longed for things to be different between us. I needed to know that he wanted me, but I respected myself enough not to ask for it. I couldn't accept things the way they were anymore.

I turned to Lily and said, "Lily… I'm so sorry about

the accident. I don't know what happened, but you have to know I would never do anything to hurt John Warren. I love that little guy."

"Stop, Courtney, I know you would never do anything to hurt him. We all know that. This wasn't your fault. Bobby will explain everything to you later."

"I hate that I can't remember anything. It's driving me crazy," I told her.

She sat in the chair beside me and glanced over to me with a look of such sadness it made me want to cry. "It was bad, Courtney. We were worried that you weren't going to wake up. You really had us scared. Poor Bobby has been a wreck. He hasn't left your side the entire time."

"Can we please talk about something else for a little while?" I asked. "I'd rather hear about everything I've missed."

She gave me a questioning look but didn't push. Instead, she smiled and said, "Girl, I don't know where to start. Tessa will be here a little later.... Izzie has a really high fever, and Tessa thinks she has the flu. She took her to the doctor to get tested."

"That's awful. Please tell her to call and let me know how she's doing," I told her.

"I will. Umm... I guess you didn't know that she asked Bishop to postpone the wedding until you were out of the hospital...."

"What? No, I didn't know that!" I screeched.

"She told him that she just couldn't do it without you," Lily said.

"I can't believe she actually postponed the wedding! She was so excited! Now I feel like I messed everything up for her," I told her regretfully.

"Don't be silly. None of this was your fault. Tessa couldn't bear the thought of not having you by her side. It just wouldn't be the same without you there," Lily told me reassuringly.

"I don't know about that. I'm sure Bishop would have liked it to be just them, but Tessa is worth the wait. So tell me... what's going on with you and Goliath?"

"Things couldn't be better. John Warren's biological father, Maverick, found us, and let's just say it was *complicated*. He eventually decided that John Warren is safer here with us, so he's going to let him stay. We've even made plans to adopt him."

She looked over to the door to make sure no one was there, and then quickly turned to me. A wide smile spread across her face as she leaned in and whispered, "I have a little secret. I'm not sure if it's okay to tell yet, but I have to tell someone."

"I love secrets. You can tell me.... I won't tell a soul! It's in the vault!" I said as I brought my fingers up to my mouth and pretended to zip my lips.

"It's still really early, but... I'm pregnant! Goliath and I are going to have a baby! Can you believe that?" Her eyes gleamed with excitement as she shared her news with me. Lily was such a special person, and I was truly happy for them.

"Goliath is going to make a great dad, Lily. He's been so wonderful with John Warren. I'm sure he's thrilled."

"He is. He's already talking about finding us a new place to live. He wants us to move into a bigger house at the end of the month."

"I'm so happy that everything is working out so well for you two. You really are perfect together."

"Is everything okay with you and Bobby? You know you can talk to me. I can tell something is up, because normally you never want him to leave your side," she ventured.

"I really can't explain it, Lily. It's like this whole accident thing made me see everything so differently. I could've died. It's made me realize that life's too short. I'm tired of wasting time on something that just isn't going to happen," I told her.

"Courtney, you've been through *a lot*. Give yourself some time to sort this all out before you make any rash decisions you might regret later."

"That's just it. I've given it time... too much time. You know as well as I do that the men in this club don't let things stand in their way. They know what they want, and they go after it. *Nothing* gets in their way."

"I know it looks that way, but there's so much more to it. You can't compare your relationship to others'. Bobby loves you. Everyone knows that."

"I know he cares about me, but that's not enough. Bobby's never shown me that I'm the one for him. I can't do it anymore," I told her. I couldn't believe that I'd actually said it out loud. As hard as it would be to let him go, I knew I had to do it.

"I don't know what to…" Lily started before Bobby suddenly walked back into the room.

"How's she doing?" he asked Lily.

"I'm fine, Bobby," I said, answering for her.

"Um, I really need to get going guys. Goliath has plans for us this afternoon, but I'll be back soon." Lily quickly stood up and leaned over to give me another hug. "Call me if you need anything," she whispered before heading for the door.

"I will. Thanks so much for coming. It really meant a lot to me," I told her.

Lily smiled as she walked out of the room. She looked so happy. I had to give Goliath credit. He was completely committed to Lily, and he wasn't afraid to show it. That's the way it should be. I took a deep breath and tried to find the right words to say to Bobby.

"You doing okay?" he asked.

"I'm okay," I told him. Physically, I really felt fine, despite being in a coma for the past ten days. It was my heart that was having the problem. I knew what I needed to do, but it was just going to be hard to follow through with it.

Bobby reached for my hand and said, "I know this is a lot, Court. We'll get…."

"*Don't*, Bobby. Really, just don't." I turned my head and faced the wall. Just looking at him hurt me too much. I wanted to be strong and do what I knew I needed to do. Why did it have to be so difficult?

"What? *Tell me*. Exactly what the hell is going on in that head of yours?" he asked with frustration. I didn't answer him right away, and I could feel the tension building between us with every second that passed. "Court?"

I looked him in the eye and said, "You know, I've heard that going through a traumatic experience can change you, but I've never really believed it until now. I've finally seen things for what they are."

"What do you mean?" Bobby asked.

"This thing between you and me. I'm done, Bobby," I stated harshly as I motioned my hand between us.

"Just like that? You wake up from being in a coma all this time, and now you think you have it all figured out?" he asked, his voice laced with confusion and anger.

"As a matter of fact, yes. I'd say this thing between you and me is over, but the truth is, it never really started."

"You're wrong. Now stop. You're mine, Courtney," he said as he reached for my hand. "You always have been, and you always will be."

"I was never yours, Bobby. You and I both know that," I said as I snatched my hand away.

"That's bullshit. You're mine in *every* fucking way, Courtney," Bobby snapped. He sighed deeply as he raked his fingers through his hair.

I took a deep breath and tried to look him in the eye as I said, "I don't want to argue with you. It's a simple fact. A man knows what he wants. I wasn't it for you. I'm okay with that, but it's time for us to move on. It took having this accident for me to realize that I want more. I want a man that wants me without any doubts or reservations."

"You're wrong, Courtney! Totally fucking wrong. You're it for me!" he pleaded. He leaned over me and pressed his lips against mine. My heart ached as I placed my hands on his chest pushing him away.

"Please, stop. Just go, Bobby!" I shouted as I shook my head.

He was about to say something when the nurse rushed in. "What's going on in here?"

"Nothing!" Bobby snapped.

"We could hear you shouting in the hallway. Sir, I'm going to have to ask you to leave," she demanded.

"I'm not going anywhere," he said angrily.

"Bobby, just go. I *need* you to go," I pleaded as I fought back the tears that threatened to betray my feelings.

The nurse stepped between us and started to usher Bobby out of the room. Before he left, he turned to me and said, "This isn't over. I'm not giving you up."

Tears streamed down my face as I watched him walk towards the door, but I knew I was making the right decision. I had given him enough time, and I wasn't willing to give him any more. Something inside me had broken with the accident. I didn't know what. I just knew that nothing between us was the same. The accident had changed me forever.

CHAPTER 2

Real loss only occurs when you lose something that
you love more than yourself.

Anonymous

BOBBY

EVERYTHING WAS FUCKED up, and it was all my
goddamn fault. Courtney had every right to be
pissed at me. I'd failed her in more ways than I could
count. Not claiming her when I'd had the chance was
just one of many things. She would never have been in
that fucking hospital if it weren't for me. She was right to
push me away. I'd never be the man that she deserved,
but that didn't mean I was going to let her go. I'd give
her the time she needed, but I would fix this thing
between us no matter what it took. She was mine, and I
planned to make sure she knew it.

After spending a restless night at home, I decided the
most important thing I had to do was make sure
Courtney was safe. There was no way I would ever let
anything happen to her again. I decided to get to the
clubhouse and see if there were any new leads on the

Black Diamonds. I got all the surveillance equipment ready to install at their clubhouse and loaded it up in the back of Bishop's SUV. Then, I texted Goliath and Renegade to let them know everything was ready.

We got to their clubhouse well after midnight. I wanted a good view of the place without getting too close, so I used the long distance lenses on our cameras. After we installed those, I had to get close enough to install the splitter. It enabled us to stream directly from the cameras they'd already installed inside their clubhouse. It was 3:00 a.m., and by that time most of the Black Diamonds had left the compound or crashed for the night. Goliath and Renegade stood watch as I found the line to their main security system. Once I disabled it, we made our way to the camera feed that led to the inside of the club. After I checked to make sure the splitter was working, we re-enabled their security system and headed home.

Since it was so late and I was exhausted, I decided to stay at my room at the clubhouse. I didn't want to go home and face that empty fucking house. Just the thought of it felt like a punch in the gut. I had almost made it to my room when Cindy stepped out of the bathroom. Fuck. I was not in the mood to deal with her shit tonight. I didn't speak and tried to walk right past her.

"Where are you rushing off to?" she asked seductively as she blocked my way. Her hand trailed down my arm as she spoke.

"To *sleep*," I told her as I removed her hand from my

arm, wishing she would take the hint and go away.

"Want some company?" she asked as she stepped closer to me. No such luck. I was so over her bullshit. I wished I'd never made the mistake of fucking her in the first place. She didn't know when to just let it go.

"Don't start that shit tonight, Cindy. You know the answer is *no*. It's always been no, and nothing is going to change that," I told her as I opened my door.

"I doubt that, but no worries, Honey. I'll be around when you change your mind," she whispered.

I didn't respond. I slammed the door behind me and crashed into my bed. I had barely closed my eyes when thoughts of Courtney forced their way into my head. The bed seemed so big without her lying there next to me. I missed the warmth of her body pressed against mine. I couldn't get her off my mind, so I reached into the dresser beside my bed and grabbed a large bottle of scotch. In a matter of minutes, I had drained the entire bottle. I hoped it would take the edge off and ease the tightness in my chest. Thankfully, it didn't take long for it to go into effect. I finally let my exhaustion take over and passed out.

The next day, I woke up later than I'd planned, and my head was pounding. I went to the kitchen to grab some aspirin and get something to eat. Bishop was standing there talking on his burner cell, and he looked pissed as he listened to what was being said on the other end of the line. With a demanding voice he said, "I *absolutely* think we should meet. We have lots to discuss." He was silent for a moment before he said, "We'll be there." He hung up his phone and placed it in his back pocket as he shook his head.

"Something up?" I asked.

"Snake wants a meet. There's some shit going down with his club, and he thinks we have something to do with it. It's good, though. I've got some questions of my own, so I have no problem meeting up with him," Bishop said flatly.

"Why would we have anything to do with what's going on at his club?" I asked.

"No fucking idea, but I'll find out everything later tonight. I want you and Goliath to be there."

"No problem. By the way, we got the surveillance set up at the Black Diamond's warehouse last night. I'll pull up the feed, so we can get an update about what's going on over there."

"Good. Let me know what…" he started but got distracted as his phone started ringing. Just as he was reaching into his pocket, Sheppard rushed in the front door.

"You need to get home. Something happened with Myles," Sheppard shouted. The color drained from Bishop's face at the mention of his son's name. Myles was Bishop's only child, and they'd always been very close.

"Tessa's been trying to call you, but she couldn't get through," Sheppard told him.

Bishop looked down at his phone and answered it as he charged towards the door. "I'm on my way," he barked into the phone.

Sheppard and I followed him over to his house. An ambulance and several neighbors lined his driveway. Tessa was talking to one of the paramedics that were working on Myles, and it was obvious that she'd been crying. Bishop rushed over to them as Sheppard and I followed close behind. Tessa began sobbing again as soon as she saw him. He wrapped his arm around her and led her towards the ambulance to ask one of the paramedics, "How is my son?"

"He has some minor lacerations and a broken wrist. He'll need to have it x-rayed as soon as possible."

"Myles, you doing okay?" Bishop asked.

"Yes, sir. I'm fine," Myles replied sounding embarrassed.

"I'll let them finish checking you over, and then we'll go see about your wrist," Bishop told him. Myles nodded and sat patiently as the paramedics finished wrapping his wrist.

Bishop turned to Tessa and asked, "What happened?"

"It all happened so fast. I tried, but I couldn't get to him in time," Tessa cried hysterically.

Bishop pulled her close to him and waited for her to calm down. Once she was able to pull it together, she continued, "I was putting the Christmas decorations in the garage when he decided he wanted to ride his dirt bike in the field across the street. He'd barely pulled out onto the road when all these motorcycles came racing up next to him. He lost his balance and crashed into the bank," she said as she brushed the tears from her eyes.

"They meant to do it, Bishop. They tried to hurt him!"

Bishop continued to hold her close as he said, "It's going to be okay, Tess. We'll figure all this out."

Goliath pulled up while Bishop was talking to Tessa. He came over to me and asked, "Is he okay?"

"He's banged up a little, but I think he's gonna be alright," I told him.

"Sheppard said some guys ran him off the road. Do we know who it was?" he asked.

"Tessa isn't sure, but I'd lay odds it's the same guys who hurt Courtney," I told him.

"Fuck!" Goliath growled, his face filling with rage. "Women and children? What kind of fucking scum are we dealing with?"

"These guys have no code, Goliath. They don't care who they hurt as long as they get their point across. I have a feeling you were their original target," I told him.

"I was thinking the same damn thing. Courtney's accident wasn't some random attack. They were trying to get to me through John Warren. I'm going to bring those motherfuckers to their knees."

"Now you know how I've been feeling the past few weeks," I told him sarcastically.

"I've known all along, Crack Nut. I've always planned to make them pay, but now I want to get them even more. We'll get them. No doubt about that," Goliath snapped.

"Hopefully we'll get more information when we meet up with Snake tonight."

"Looking forward to it. Lily told me that Courtney

was doing better and might be coming home soon. At least that's good news."

"Yeah, it's good news." Fuck. It should've been the best goddamn news ever. I hated that I wasn't going to be there with her when she came home.

Bishop was done talking to Tessa, so he headed over to us. "We're going on lockdown. Get everyone to the clubhouse. No one leaves until I give the word."

"What about Courtney?" I asked.

"Already thought of that. Goliath put one of the prospects on her until she's released from the hospital." He didn't wait for my response before he turned and went back over to Myles and Tessa. I wasn't happy about the arrangement, but it would have to do.

"I'll make the call. I'll see you back over at the clubhouse. You'll need to be ready in a couple of hours," Bishop called over his shoulder.

"I'll be ready," I told him.

CHAPTER 3

COURTNEY

I T'D BEEN FOREVER since I'd seen anyone other than my parents, and I was about to go batshit crazy. They'd been there every day pacing back and forth in that tiny room, rambling on and on about this or that. To make matters worse, my mother was constantly fussing over me. I was going to blow a gasket if she tried to fix my pillow one more time. I was on the brink of losing my sanity, and truthfully, my dad wasn't much better. He sat in his chair mumbling and griping about Bobby. He completely blamed him for the accident, and no matter what I said, he just wouldn't listen to me. I'd finally had all I could take and begged them to go home. I was shocked but relieved when they actually decided to leave.

Then, I was stuck in the room alone with my thoughts, and like a complete idiot, I couldn't stop thinking about Bobby. His handsome face taunted me every time I closed my eyes. He was one of those guys that was just naturally attractive. He didn't spend hours in the gym and think about the clothes he wore. It just came easily to him. I didn't like the fact that his sandy blonde hair had grown over the past few weeks, because it made it hard to see his beautiful brown eyes. Damn it. I had to stop thinking about him. I missed him so much that I was starting to have second thoughts about breaking things off. I was a mess, and all my doubts were bouncing around inside my head.

The fact was, I'd never loved anyone like I loved him, and it was hard to let him go. I wondered if I would ever feel that way about someone again. It didn't help matters when the nurse told me he'd been calling several times a day to check on me. I needed to stop thinking about him. I'd made my decision, and I had to throw on my big girl panties and live with it. *Crap.* I needed to get out of that damn hospital room before I completely lost my ever-loving mind!

I was stuck, though. The doctors wanted to keep me for a few days to monitor my progress. Over the past few weeks, I'd lost some muscle tone, and they'd told me it might take some time to build my strength back up. Truthfully, I was feeling pretty good and didn't think it would take me long to get back on my feet.

Tessa called several times, and that helped distract me for a little while. She apologized over and over for not being there with me. Apparently the club was on some sort of lockdown, whatever that meant. They'd even sent one of their "prospector guys" to stand outside my door. Something had happened with Myles, but Tessa wouldn't tell me much about it. I knew it had something to do with the club, but I didn't push her to tell me. I'd learned not to ask. She would've told me if she could.

Several days later, Bishop finally brought her by to see me. I was so excited. I felt like we hadn't seen each other in months, and I missed her more than I'd realized. She was my best friend and had always helped me through the hard times in my life. I needed her then more than ever. After being cooped up in that hospital bed for so long, she was my lifeline to the outside world.

"Hey there, sweetie! How are you feeling?" she asked as she raced over and gave me a big hug.

"Better now. It's so good to see you! I'm about to lose my mind in this place. I've missed you all so much," I told her.

"I'm so sorry that I haven't been by sooner. The doctors didn't want me to expose you to the flu. Izzie was really sick, and none of us wanted to risk it," she told me.

"I hate that she was sick. Is she feeling better?" I asked.

"Yes, much better, finally. Now we just need to get through this whole lockdown thing. It has been a total nightmare," she said with frustration.

"Does the lockdown have anything to do with the guy that's been standing outside my door the past few days?" I asked.

"Well… yeah. That's Levi. He's one of the prospects from the club. I can't really go into it, but it's for your safety. There will be someone else coming to take his place when you're released from the hospital."

"*Seriously?* Is that really necessary? It's not like Bobby and I are still together," I told her.

"I know, honey, but we all consider you part of the family. And you know, Bishop is all about protecting his family," she said, her pride evident in her smile.

"Well, Mr. Hot-in-Leather is being overprotective. I don't think he has anything to worry about with me." Tessa just shook her head and laughed. She knew it was true. Bishop was totally hot, and I loved picking on her about it. "So, who are they sending to babysit me?" I asked.

"Well, ummm…" she stammered.

"Do not say Bobby, Tess. You know I need my distance from him right now. I know we'll have to cross paths eventually, but I'm gonna need some space right now," I told her.

"It's not Bobby, Court. Bishop knew you wouldn't want him to do it. I can't really go into all the details… but John Warren's dad, Maverick, is going to be staying here for a while, and Bishop thought he'd be…."

"Maverick? Wait, no. I don't know anything about the guy!"

"It'll be fine. You'll really like him, Court. Something bad was going on in his club back in Washington, and he needed a place to lay low," Tessa explained.

"Ha! Lay low? Look at you talking all Biker Bitch," I told her, laughing. The truth was I really didn't care who they chose to watch over me as long as it wasn't Bobby. I thought it might actually be nice to have something to take my mind off of things, and maybe Maverick would be just the distraction that I needed. "It's fine. I trust Bishop, and I know he wouldn't ask Maverick to do this if he didn't trust him."

"Bishop cleared him. It might be a little weird having him there at first. Just remember, he'll be there to watch over you and make sure you're safe. Do what he says, and everything will be fine," Tessa said with a warning in her voice. I knew she was worried about me, so I'd do whatever they needed me to.

"Besides, Lily said that he's really sweet. You might just end up liking him," Tessa said as she brushed her hair behind her ear.

"Don't even think about it. No more bikers for me. Besides, I need time to get myself together. I might even take some online classes," I told her, trying to change the subject.

"That sounds like a great idea. You should do that."

"I need to get out of here first, and school starts back next week. I have so much to do," I told her.

"Don't rush things. You need time to get back to your old self. Besides, Bishop may not want you going back to work yet," Tessa said with concern.

"Why not?" I asked.

"It may not be safe for either of us to go. We'll have to wait and see what he says. He'll do whatever it takes to keep us out of danger, and you could always use the extra time to get back on your feet," Tessa replied.

"Maybe you're right, but I need a distraction. The kids would keep my mind off of things with Bobby," I told her.

"You know, Bobby hasn't been himself the last few days. Are you sure...?"

"Yep, so don't start with the motherly advice thing you do. I know I did the right thing. It's just gonna be hard for a while. I miss him... *a lot*, but I can't keep making the same mistakes over and over again. It's time to grow up and stop wishing for things that aren't gonna happen. Now, how's Myles?"

"He's fine. He was a little upset about what happened, but he's doing better. His wrist was fractured, but it wasn't bad. They gave him a brace to wear for a few weeks," she explained. She still didn't tell me exactly what had happened, but I could tell she was really freaked out about it.

"Tell him I'm thinking about him. I miss everybody so much. I can't wait to see Drake and Izzie. It's been too long."

"The kids miss you, too. They ask about you all the time. We'll have movie night as soon as you get home," Tessa promised.

"I'd really like that."

Bishop tapped on the door before he walked in. He gave me one of his sexy smiles before he said, "Hey there, stranger. Nice to have you back."

"It's nice to be back," I told him.

"Tessa tell you about Maverick?" he asked.

"Yep. I don't think all that is necessary, but I know you do. So... I'll roll with it."

"Good. You're club, Court. I don't know why this happened, but you have my word, nothing will happen

30

to you again. We will protect you. Be sure to give us a call when the doctor releases you. I want Maverick to go over and check out your place before you get there."

"Okay. Fingers crossed that they'll let me go home tomorrow, and then I want a movie marathon with the kids," I pleaded.

"You got it." Tessa leaned over and gave me another hug. "I'll see you soon. Love ya, girl."

"Love you, too. Take care of her, Bishop."

"You know I will," he said as he reached for her hand. The room seemed so empty as soon as they walked out. I reached for the remote and tried to find something to watch. I was in dire need of a scary movie—the freakier the better. I was flipping through the channels when a group of motorcycles crossed the screen. I froze. My heart stopped for a minute as the memories of my accident came rushing back to me.

"You ready to go, little man? We better get going, or Lily is going to think I've run off with you," I told him as I lifted him out of his high chair. I quickly changed his diaper and slipped on his warm clothes. The temperature had really dropped over the past few days, and I didn't want him to get cold.

"I know you hate wearing hats, sweetie, but you're gonna need it. Trust me on this one," I told him as I slipped the small toboggan over his head. I zipped up his coat and placed him in his car seat. I carefully lifted the carrier and threw his diaper bag over my shoulder as I walked out the door. Once I got him settled in the car, I started the engine and eased out of the driveway. I hadn't driven far when I noticed bright lights in the rearview mirror.

When I looked closer, I saw that the lights were coming from several motorcycles. At first, I assumed it was just the guys heading to the clubhouse, but I quickly realized that I was wrong. I didn't know those men, and they were driving really close to my car. Too close.

My heart started to race when I looked over to my side window and saw the handles of a motorcycle near my car door. Panic surged through me as I saw the dark eyes of a strange man staring right at me. I'd never seen him before—I would have remembered seeing him. He had one of those faces a girl could never forget. He gave me wicked smile as he steered his bike closer and closer to my car. Two more bikes pulled around to the front of my car, and the three bikes behind me started pulling up to the side.

"Oh god! John Warren… hold on, baby. I'm gonna try to get away from them. It's going to be okay," I told him, trying to sound calmer than I really was. I was just a few miles from the clubhouse. Surely I could just speed up, and they would give up and leave me alone. I pushed the gas pedal, but the man beside me eased closer and started to shake his head. He reached into his side pocket and pulled out a gun. A gun! I was in shock. The whole world seemed to freeze in that moment. I couldn't take my eyes off of him. What the hell was he doing? I couldn't understand why he was doing this to me. He continued to smile at me as he pointed the gun in my direction. A thousand thoughts rushed through my head as I looked at the barrel of the gun. I held my breath and waited for him to pull the trigger.

It all happened so fast. I couldn't do anything to stop it. The steering wheel shook, and the sound of crashing metal filled the small space of the car. It was so loud—like a diesel truck slamming into a concrete wall. I felt my body lift from the seat as *the car flipped high into the air. Everything moved in slow motion. I watched the car break apart as it crashed into the ground over and over. John Warren began to cry, and my heart broke. I wanted to cover him, protect him, but I couldn't reach him. I couldn't even call out his name. I was totally powerless. I gripped the steering wheel with all my strength as the car continued to crash down into the deep ravine. There was nothing I could do to stop it. I prayed that John Warren would be okay. I clenched my jaw and felt my body tense as I was jarred from side to side in my seat. Even with my seatbelt, I felt like I was being tossed around like a rag doll. Then, as quickly as it had started, it all ended. Everything went silent. Totally and absolutely silent.*

My heart was racing, and the tightness in my chest made it hard to breathe. Panic surged through me as the memory of what happened raced through my mind. Those men tried to kill me. It wasn't an accident at all. It was finally all coming together, and I didn't like it. I didn't like it one damn bit.

CHAPTER 4

The most powerful weapon on Earth
is the human soul on fire.
Ferdinand Foch

BOBBY

—————◆◇◆—————

I HATED BEING on lockdown. It made the one place I loved seem like a goddamned prison. The tension levels were building among the brothers, and supplies were running low. Sheppard and Otis had taken Cindy and Brandie to load up on groceries and liquor, but we'd gone through most of that in the first few days. I was getting stir crazy. I hadn't been out of the place since the night we'd met with Snake.

It was over a week ago when we'd met up with him in a hole-in-the-wall biker bar outside of Murray, Kentucky. They said it was considered neutral territory, so Bishop agreed to the location.

Snake wasn't there when we arrived, so we sat at a small table at the back corner of the bar and placed our order. The waitress had just brought over our beers when Snake and two of his men walked in. None of them spoke as they made their way over to us. Snake didn't look like a happy man. Without saying a word, they sat down at the table. The tattoo on Snake's neck pulsed as he glared at Bishop. I didn't have a good feeling about what was about to go down.

He gave Bishop a harsh look and said, "You wanna tell me how the Black Diamonds know I talked to you? We got a war on our hands, brother?"

"You got it wrong, man. No one outside of my club knows that I've even spoken to you. You gonna tell me what the hell is going on?" Bishop snapped.

"Two days after I called you, those motherfuckers started causing all kinds of problems in *my* town. Today, they ran my VP's sixteen year old daughter off the road and almost killed her."

"They're playing the same shit with us. First, it was my VP's son and his sitter, and today it was my son," Bishop told him.

"Looks like they're going after the kids. Lowlife motherfuckers got no code. Women and children are off limits," Snake said as his face flashed with anger. "Doesn't matter. They've fucked with the wrong goddamn club now. There's no fucking way I'm gonna let them pull this shit," he barked as he slammed his fist against the table.

"How did you get word that they were coming to Paris?" Bishop asked.

"There'd been talk among the other charters about the Black Diamonds expanding their territory. Some even thought our club had ties to 'em, trying to branch out with them. Word was they were looking to the Tennessee River to transport their weapons."

"There are over 2,000 barges that move along that river," Bishop told him.

"And they planned to use 'em. If they played it right, they could distribute their weapons across three states," Snake said as he pulled his pack of cigarettes out of his front pocket. He lit a cigarette, and after taking a long drag, he said, "It didn't take much to put two and two together. That's when I gave you a call. Wasn't even sure they'd head your way."

"There has to be more to it than that. Seems to me these guys have some kind of grudge," Bishop said with concern.

"I don't give a fuck what kind of *grudge* they got. They think they can do this shit in my town?" he said shaking his head. "Not gonna fucking happen. I'll take those motherfuckers down."

"We have a few leads, but we need to have an understanding before I share," Bishop demanded.

"What do you have in mind, brother?" Snake asked suspiciously.

"We need an alliance. We work together to bring down these fucking Black Diamonds," Bishop said as he sat back and crossed his arms over his chest.

"Consider it done," Snake replied with a nod. "I look forward to making these fuckers weep."

"We need to play this smart, Snake. They're coming after our families, and I intend to do whatever it takes to keep them safe," Bishop said with concern in his voice.

"You got my word, Bishop."

We talked for over an hour and shared everything we knew. We didn't gain a great deal of new information, but we did secure some help. Snake made it clear that he had no intention of going easy on those guys. He wanted them taken care of by any means necessary. We'd have to decide as a club how we would pursue it. We'd worked too hard to clean up our club to throw it all away dealing with scum like the Black Diamonds.

Bishop had called for church as soon as we got back home so he could let the others know what we'd found out during our meet with Snake. Nothing had really happened since then. The club was still under lockdown, so I spent my time searching through the security feed from the Black Diamonds' clubhouse. There was some talk about an upcoming delivery in Northern Kentucky, but they hadn't mentioned any specific details yet.

I was getting restless. Courtney appeared in my every thought. It had been over a week since I'd walked out of that hospital room, and it was killing me. I'd checked with her nurse every day to see how she was doing and found out that she was about to be released.

Bishop had sent Maverick over to her house to check things over. He'd needed to check her place out and make sure everything was ready for her when she got home. Bishop also sent Brandie to pick up groceries and whatever else they would need when Courtney got home. The whole situation made me feel uneasy. I had to admit that after getting to know Maverick during lockdown, he seemed like a nice enough guy. That didn't mean that I was happy about him being with Courtney twenty-four hours a day, though. It was hard to accept that I wasn't going to be the one taking care of her. It didn't matter who was there. I knew it should've been me. Regardless, I had to trust that Bishop knew what he was doing. He'd cleared Maverick and believed he was the right guy for the job. Nevertheless, I planned to keep an eye on things. I needed to know for myself that everything was okay with Courtney. She was my woman, and I planned to do whatever it took to keep her out of harm's way.

CHAPTER 5

COURTNEY

~~~~~~•◦◦◦•~~~~~~

I PACED AROUND my hospital room, gathering up my belongings, feeling relieved that I was finally being released. Everyone had been so nice, but I felt like the walls were about to close in on me. I was ready to get the hell out of there. I should've called my parents, but I'd decided not to let them know I was being discharged. I felt a little guilty about it, but I just wasn't up for all the melodramatics. Mom would've been a nervous wreck hovering over me every two seconds, and my dad would've run around the house trying to fix stuff that didn't really need to be fixed. I just didn't have the patience to deal with all that on my first day back at home.

As I packed, there was a knock on my door. Instead of waiting for me to answer, a man I'd never met before just walked right in. He stood by the door and stared at me with a curious look on his face. I stared back, trying to figure out if I knew him. After a few seconds, I realized he had to be Maverick. There was no mistaking those gorgeous green eyes. They looked just like JW's. I smiled, but I got no response from him. I couldn't figure out why he was looking at me that way. It was like he couldn't decide what to say... or that he smelled something really bad. I couldn't tell.

"What?" I asked sharply.

"You're Courtney, right?" he asked as he cocked his head to the side.

"Yep, that'd be me. I take it you're Maverick?"

"Yeah, I'm Maverick," he said as he shook his head. From his facial expression, I could tell he was mulling something over.

"*What?*" I asked impatiently. "Is something wrong?"

"No, nothing's wrong. You just aren't what I expected." He took a step closer to me and continued, "For a girl that just got out of a coma, I wouldn't expect you to be so beautiful."

"I don't know if I should take that as a compliment or not," I told him.

"You should," he said with a smirk. "Tessa and Lily told me a lot about you. Seems like the next few weeks are going to be... interesting."

"Well, now you have me curious. What exactly did my *friends* tell you about me?" I asked.

"Let's see..." he said with a big grin. He crossed his arms across his chest before he continued, "You have a thing for scary movies, but only if you have the right snacks. You love to dance, you tend to get out of hand when you drink too much, and you fidget and talk a lot when you get nervous. They also mentioned that you have a problem with texting and driving. There's more, but you get the idea."

"Damn," I said as I felt the rush of heat creep across my face. I placed my hands on my hips and looked to the ground to hide my blushing. "I'd say my girls know me pretty well."

"Yep. So... you ready to bust out of here, Cheeks?" he asked with a sexy smile.

"Absolutely," I told him smiling back. *Cheeks?* Oh well. Guess I didn't hide the blushing thing after all. I shook my head as I packed the last of my things into my overnight bag. Maverick picked it up and headed for the door. I decided that having him around might not be that bad after all. He actually did seem to be nice, and it didn't hurt that he was good looking. That scruffy look, with his day old beard and shaggy brown hair, worked for him. Under different circumstances, I could've even seen myself falling for a guy like him. Sadly, just the thought of being with another man made my heart ache. There was no denying the fact that I still missed Bobby. Hopefully having Maverick around would help me keep my mind off of him for a while.

Once we were in his truck and heading to my house, I turned to him. "So, how is this whole thing going to work?" I asked.

"I'll do my best to stay out of your way, but I'm here to keep you safe. I'll do whatever it takes to make sure no harm comes to you," Maverick said seriously. Serious Maverick was sexy. I liked *serious* Maverick.

"Will you be staying at my house?" I asked.

"Yeah. You're stuck with me for now. Hopefully it

won't be too bad, though. I'll stay in your guest room until this thing blows over."

"How long do you think this *thing* is gonna take?" I asked.

"You ready to get rid of me already?" he asked laughing.

"That's not it at all. I just hate putting you out like this. I'm sure you have more important things to do than babysit me."

"Right now, keeping you safe *is* the most important thing to me. Besides, being here will give me a chance to spend some time with John Warren." As he turned into my driveway he said, "Now, let's get you settled, and I'll make us some dinner."

"That sounds great. I'm sick of hospital food. There's only so much Jell-O a girl can eat."

When we walked into the house, the first thing I noticed were the flames glowing in the fireplace. Damn. My thoughts went straight to Bobby. He always made sure to light a fire for us whenever it was cold outside. It was just one of those little things he did that meant so much to me.

As I walked further into the living room, I saw Bobby's red fleece blanket folded at the end of the sofa. He would make fun of me every time I curled up with that old blanket. I'd even tried to steal it from him on more than one occasion, but he always ended up taking it back to his house. He said it was the only way he could make me stay at his place. There was no denying it. Bobby had been there, but I tried not to make a big deal out of it. I shook my head and followed Maverick as he carried my bag to my room.

He put it on the dresser and said, "Why don't you get settled while I go get dinner ready?" he asked.

"That sounds good," I replied as he turned and headed for the kitchen.

I felt such a sense of relief just being back in my own room. It felt so good to be home. I wanted to crawl into my bed and try to forget everything that had happened over the past few weeks. I pulled the covers back on my bed and found a square box sitting on the pillow. I picked it up and slowly opened it. It was a new iPad with a note from Bobby.

> *Thought this might make your time at home go by a little faster.*
> *Love, Bobby*

I stared at it for a few minutes, almost scared to see what was on it. I pressed the power button, and the main screen filled with tons of my favorite movies. He'd even found several that I'd told him I wanted to see but hadn't been able to find. It also had some of my favorite magazines and songs downloaded on it. Damn it. Why did he have to be so stinking thoughtful? I tossed it to the other side of the bed and tried to block it from my thoughts, but I couldn't help it. I felt the smile slowly spread across my face as I thought about how sweet it was of Bobby to do that. I couldn't believe he'd taken the time to do something like that for me. *Get your shit together, Courtney!* I shook my head, trying to clear Bobby from my mind.

I took a deep breath and decided I needed a hot bath. It was the perfect way to end a crazy day. I walked into my bathroom, and then stopped in utter shock. My pulse quickened, and I could feel my chest tighten as I slowly reached out for Bobby's t-shirt that was folded on the sink. It was the shirt I'd always worn when I stayed at his place. Oh, *hell no.* I shook my head as I tossed that sucker clear across the room. He was playing hardball, and I wasn't going to let him get to me. It was going to take more than a few movies and an old damn t-shirt to change my mind.

A few hours later, Maverick called me into the kitchen. He'd made my favorite Italian pasta for dinner. I was impressed. The table was set, and it smelled incredible. It turned out to be the best chicken alfredo I'd ever eaten. We talked all through dinner. I was amazed at how easy he was to talk to. It was like we'd know each other forever. Without thinking, I blurted out, "I remembered what happened the night of the accident."

He leaned back in his chair and looked at me thoughtfully. "You wanna tell me about it?"

"I couldn't remember anything at first. It was so frustrating laying in that damn hospital and not knowing what really happened. I tried to remember, but everything was just a haze. Then, it came rushing back to me all at once. Truthfully… I wish I hadn't remembered." I spent the next half hour telling him everything I could recall.

"Can you tell me about the guy that came up to your window? What did he look like?" he asked.

"It was dark, but I could still see this large, jagged scar that went down the entire side of his face. I don't think I'll ever forget it. His long hair was pulled back into a ponytail, and he had one of those beards like old guys wear. He gave me the creeps."

"Any idea how many guys were with him?"

"At least six, maybe seven."

"You did good, Courtney. I need to call Bishop. It'll help him know which guy he's looking for," Maverick said.

"Why do you think they were going after me? I'm really not part of the club. I know I was dating Bobby, but we weren't official or anything."

"There's more to it than that, but I can't go into it with you right now. Just know that we're going to do everything we can to make sure it doesn't happen again."

"I guess I'll have to take your word for it. I hate that I don't know what's going on. Will you at least tell me if I need to be worried?" I asked.

"There's nothing for you to worry about. I got this, and with Bobby's security system, nothing will get by us. I'm going to give Bishop a call. Let me know if you remember anything else," he said compassionately.

Just the mention of Bobby's name made my heart sink. I had totally forgotten about the security system he had installed a few months ago. He was so determined to make sure the house was safe, and at the time, I thought it meant that he loved me. I wasn't so sure anymore.

"You okay?" Maverick asked.

"I'm just tired. I think I'm going to call it a night," I told him. I put my dishes in the sink and before I left the kitchen, I turned to him and said, "Thank you, Maverick. I really do appreciate everything. It means a lot."

"No thanks needed, Courtney. I enjoyed it. Just give me a shout if you need anything," Maverick said with a smile.

"Will do. 'Nite."

"Goodnight," Maverick said as I walked out of the room. I got in the bed and pulled the covers over me. I wasn't in the mood to watch TV, so I turned off the lights and tried to focus on getting some sleep. I had just gotten comfortable when my phone beeped with a text message. I reached over to the nightstand and grabbed it from my purse. It was a message from Bobby.

Bobby: *Good night, Court. Miss you*

It was a simple message, but it brought a thousand questions to my mind. Did he know that I was home from the hospital? Did he know that I was in the bed? Did he really miss me?

CHAPTER 6

The two most powerful warriors are patience
and time.
Leo Nikolayevich Tolstoy

BOBBY

I T TOOK TWO weeks of watching the Black Diamond's surveillance video before we found something we could use. The next big shipment would be in Louisville, Kentucky in four days. The details were still sketchy, but we had a date and a location. Bishop called Snake and told him everything we had found out. They both agreed that Goliath, Renegade, and I would go with four of Snake's men to intercept the delivery. It was a risky attempt, but if we succeeded, it would send a definite message to their club.

I started skimming over all the surveillance video we had. I had to find out what time they were expecting the shipment, so we'd be able to determine the best location to intercept the delivery. It didn't take long for me to find the information I needed, but the footage gave me more questions than answers. They were up to something, but I needed more time to go through the camera footage to figure out what it was. Time I didn't have. I had to get to the garage. The guys were waiting on me to finish putting the security systems in the cars they'd remodeled.

They finished their end of the remodels days ago, and it was my turn to upgrade the security systems. Bishop wanted the new systems to enable the owner to monitor everything from their smartphone. It was pretty badass that these classic cars would have a tracking device, remote start, and a keyless entry. One of the owners even chose to include a motion-activated voice warning when people got too close his car. It was a long process, but they always seemed pleased with it in the end. Bishop needed the cars done before we left for Kentucky, so I knew it was going to be a long night.

Several of the guys were busy working in the garage, too, finishing up their own projects. I overheard Goliath talking about Lily. He was crazy about her and JW, and now that she was pregnant, he was determined to find them a new place to live. Being on lockdown was making that difficult, and he was getting frustrated.

"Lily wants to go see the house in person, but I'm not willing to risk it. We'll just have to wait until all this passes," Goliath told Bulldog.

"What's the rush?" Bull asked. "It isn't like she's gonna have that baby tomorrow."

"That's not the point. I want them in a nice place where there's actually room to move around. Her place is just too damn small," Goliath said with aggravation.

"I'm sure you'll find a place, man. Just give it time."

"That's just it. I don't want to give it time. I want those motherfuckers dealt with now. I'm tired of waiting," Goliath snapped.

"We'll get them, man. There's no doubt in my mind that they'll pay for what they tried to do to JW and Courtney. Bishop wants them just as bad as you do," Bulldog replied calmly. "You'll be set up in your new house with your kids before you know it."

They continued to yammer on back and forth about all kinds of shit that they had going on in their lives. I had to fight back the jealousy that was beginning to eat me up inside. I wanted it to be Courtney and me that were looking for a place to live. *We* should've been starting our lives together and having our own kids. The whole thing was fucked up, and I was at a loss as to how to fix it. It'd been weeks since I'd even seen her, and I was beginning to lose my patience. I'd thought that if I just gave her time, she'd realize that she was wrong about us. She hadn't, and I was starting to doubt that I'd ever get her back.

I was the only one left in the garage by the time I finished installing the last security system. Everyone else had gone to the bar to let off some steam. It was Friday, and the guys needed to get their mind off things, even if it was only for the night. I was covered in grease when I walked into the bar. I'd just planned to grab a beer and head back to my room, but that all changed the moment I saw Courtney sitting at the bar with Tessa, Lily, and Taylor. Fuck. Maverick should've told me he was bringing her over.

I went straight to my room to get cleaned up. I had to make the situation work to my advantage. After I got out of the shower, I grabbed the cologne Courtney had bought me for my birthday. I remembered her saying it was hard for her to keep her hands off of me whenever I wore it. I threw on some boxers and searched my closet for that button up shirt she liked so much. She'd already replaced the buttons on the damn thing twice. I smiled thinking about the last time she ripped it off of me. That girl had a wild side, and I couldn't wait to see her face when she saw me wearing it. I threw on a pair of jeans she liked and headed for the bar. It was time to see if I could still get a reaction out of her.

CHAPTER 7

COURTNEY

———◦◉◦———

"YOU LOOK AMAZING. It's like you were never even in the hospital," Lily said.

"Thanks, sweetie. I think I lost a little weight while I was in the coma. I can actually breathe when I wear these jeans, so I guess something good came out of it after all," I laughed. I really was feeling better, and I loved that my clothes were fitting me better. It was nice to feel good about myself again.

"Did you ever tell your parents that you were home?" Tessa asked.

"I held out as long as I could, but I finally had to tell them. They actually haven't been all that bad. They've been by to check on me a few times, but they never stay long. I think Maverick might intimidate them a little bit," I said with a shrug. Having Maverick around really did have its advantages.

"Well, I'm glad you were able to come see us tonight. We've missed you," Taylor told me.

"It was Maverick's idea. He said it would do me good to get out and have some fun before I go back to work on Monday," I told them.

"I'm looking forward to having you back at school, Court," Tessa said. "It's not the same without you there."

"I'm just relieved Bishop is letting us actually go to work," I told her.

"They decided that the kids were under a greater risk, so they're staying home for now. Bishop may be letting us go back to work, but he'll have eyes on us the entire time we're there."

"Maverick already told me, and he said I have to call and check in every hour. Before this is all over, I'm going to end up driving that man nuts."

"I doubt that, but you haven't told me yet. What do you think of Maverick?" Tessa asked with a huge smile.

"He's really nice and all, but he's just so freaking intense about *everything*. He's like my own personal drill sergeant," I told her. "It's damn near impossible to make that man smile."

"He has a lot going on. I'm sure he's worried about that stuff that's going on in his club. Has he said anything to you about it?" Lily asked.

"He's been keeping to himself lately. He's always studying the security system at the house or looking up stuff on his computer. I have no idea what he's actually looking at, but I can tell he's worried about something," I told her.

"I hope everything is going to be okay. I'd hate to see anything happen to him. I really like him, and I want John Warren to be able to get to know him," Lily said with concern.

"Don't worry too much about Maverick. I have a feeling he'll make it just fine," Tessa told her with a smile. I had to agree. Maverick seemed like the kind of guy that made things happen. I had very little doubt that he could take care of anything that got in his way.

"Enough about Mr. Serious. Tell me some good news." I turned to Lily and asked, "Has Goliath found your dream house yet?"

"Don't even get me started on that one. He's absolutely *determined* to find the perfect place, and he's driving me nuts! I've given up and just decided to let him have at it. Honestly, as long as we are together, I don't care where we live," Lily said as she passed beers over to Doc and Sheppard. They all nodded, and I watched them as they walked back over to the pool table. I smiled, thinking how much I'd liked hanging out at the club with them. Sheppard always had a way of making me laugh. I loved listening to all of his wild stories, and it didn't hurt that he was easy on the eyes. He had that boy-next-door look with his clean-cut blonde hair and blue eyes that drove the girls crazy. Doc seemed like the father figure around the club, giving advice whenever anybody would listen.

It felt nice to be there with everyone again. I hadn't realized how much I'd missed them until we all started talking. Just being with them made me feel so much better about everything. I'd been so worried about running into Bobby that I almost didn't come, but Maverick talked me into it. He reminded me that I'd have to face him sooner or later. So far, I'd been lucky. There'd been no sign of him all night.

"You ready for another beer?" Taylor asked with a smile.

"Love one," I told her. Lily reached into the cooler, only to find that it was empty.

"Damn," she said as she shook her head. "I've got to go to the back to get more beer. I'll be right back."

Before I could stop her, Bobby came up behind me and said, "I'll get it, Lily. You know Goliath will have your ass if he sees you trying to lift anything heavy." He quickly turned to leave, but I could smell a hint of his cologne as he walked away. Damn it all to hell! It was the cologne I'd bought him, and he knew it was my favorite. He'd done that on purpose. I reached over and grabbed Tessa's drink, and before she had a chance to protest, I finished it off. Tessa looked over to me with her eyebrow raised high, but I just turned my head. I didn't want to hear it. I knew something as simple as cologne shouldn't have bothered me, but it did, and I hated myself for it.

Lily motioned Bobby over to the end of the counter and showed him where to put the cases. The muscles in his arms flexed when he lowered them onto the counter. As he stepped away from the boxes, I noticed that he was wearing... the shirt. Holy hell! I couldn't believe he was wearing *the* shirt. Of all the shirts in the entire damn world he'd decided to wear *that* shirt.

"Courtney!" Tessa whispered. She placed her hand on my knee and said, "Stop shaking your leg. You're making all the bottles on the counter rattle." I just ignored her. I was too busy looking over at Bobby. Apparently he was very amused with himself. He stood there looking at me with his sly little smile. What an ass! I wanted to clock him right in the head, but I just rolled my eyes. He was getting to me, and he knew it. I had to pull my shit together.

I slowly looked back over to Tessa and said, "I'm fine. Just a little cold."

I heard Bobby cough behind me, but I didn't turn around. He knew that I was getting flustered, and it frustrated the hell out of me.

I looked over to Taylor and asked, "When are you and Renegade moving into the new house? Is it finished yet?" I asked. I watched out of the corner of my eye as Bobby walked over and joined Sheppard at the pool table. I shook my head and tried to focus on what Taylor was saying.

"Just a few more weeks. I can't wait. You should see the size of my closet!" she said excitedly. I thought it was so sweet that Renegade was building her a house out on the lake. He'd do anything for her.

"I just love the view, Taylor. It's really beautiful up there," Tessa told her.

The conversation became blurred as my attention was drawn over to the pool table. Several of the guys were playing, and I couldn't stop watching Bobby as he bent over to make his shot. I didn't know what was wrong with me. What the hell? I couldn't stop myself from staring at his ass like some sex-starved nymphomaniac!

"Courtney, you're making a mess," Tessa said as she slipped my beer out of my hand. I looked down at the small pieces of the beer label that were scattered all over the table and my lap.

"I need to go to the bathroom," I told them as I stood up to leave. "I'll be right back."

I brushed the tiny pieces of paper off my pants and headed for the bathroom. I splashed some water on my face and tried to pull myself together. I had to stop letting Bobby get to me like that. It was just a freaking shirt! I dried my hands and opened the bathroom door. My heart stopped when I found Bobby standing there. *Oh God*, I sighed under my breath.

"Court…" Bobby whispered.

I couldn't deal with him anymore. I was losing my self-control, and I needed to get the hell out of there. I took a deep breath and tried to walk past him.

After just a few steps, Bobby reached for my arm and pulled me over to him. I stumbled briefly before my body crashed into his. I felt like I was going through sensory overload as my chest pressed against his. Without thinking, my hands slowly drifted up his chest until they rested by the buttons I had just replaced a few weeks ago. I needed to resist the temptation, but I'd missed being that close to him. I rested my forehead against his chest as I waited for him to say something.

Bobby wrapped his arm around my waist, pulling me closer to him. I could feel the bristles of his beard brush against my cheek as his lips moved closer to my ear. The warmth of his breath sent chills throughout my entire body as he whispered, "I miss you."

I couldn't look at him; I'd crumble if I did. I shook my head and tried to pull myself away from him, but he had no intention of letting me go. His hands went to the side of my face. He lifted my chin, forcing me to look him in the eyes. It was just too much. His eyes lured me in, completely hypnotizing me. I hated that I wanted him as much as I did, but I couldn't deny how my body responded to him.

He lowered his mouth to mine, and I lost all my resolve and gave into him. His tongue brushed against my bottom lip, and I couldn't suppress my moan as it vibrated through my chest. He took a step forward, forcing me against the wall as he deepened the kiss. My knees became weak as he continued to claim me with his mouth. His touch consumed me, and I needed more. My hands found the back of his neck, and he grunted in approval as I raked my nails through the back of his hair. I could feel his need for me growing as his hips ground into me. My heart pounded in my chest as all the memories of us came flooding back to me. He'd been the only man I'd ever known that could get to me like that. I just couldn't help myself. I wanted that moment to change things, but I knew in my heart that it wouldn't. I brought my hands up to his chest and pushed against him, breaking the kiss.

Damn it. Why did I have to want him so much? It just wasn't fair. He looked so damn good in that stupid, stupid shirt, and… and… *shit!* I needed to get away from him. He knew I couldn't resist him, and he was playing me like a fiddle. I gave him one of my "roll over and die" looks as I turned and headed back to the bar.

I walked over to the girls and said, "I have to go. *Now*."

"What? Why?" Lily asked.

"I shouldn't have come tonight. It was just too soon," I told them. I didn't know what I'd been thinking. Bobby's pull was too strong. "I'll talk to y'all later."

I walked over to Maverick. He was sitting at the end of the bar talking to Bishop and Goliath. They all looked over to me when I walked up.

"Uh... umm... I think it's time for me to go," I told Maverick.

He nodded, and without complaint, he stood up and said his goodbyes to the guys. As we walked towards the door, I glanced back over my shoulder. Bobby was standing by the pool table with his arms crossed over his chest, and he was watching me. When our eyes met, he smiled wide and gave me a sexy wink. I could feel my face beginning to blush, so I gave the door a hard push and headed out. Well, crap. So much for playing it cool.

CHAPTER 8

Love doesn't hide. It stays and fights. It goes the distance. That's why God made love so strong. So it can carry you all the way home.

Franking P. Jones

BOBBY

W E MET FOR church Sunday night, so Bishop could reveal our plans to intercept the shipment on Tuesday. It was going to be a dangerous move, and it concerned the brothers. We'd worked hard to change the dynamic of our club, and no one wanted to jeopardize everything we'd worked for. But we didn't have a choice. The Black Diamonds were dangerous, and they would have to be dealt with—regardless of the consequences.

Goliath arranged for us to leave early Tuesday morning to meet up with four members of the Red Dragons. Bishop and Snake agreed that both clubs should be involved. We'd formed an alliance and would face them together. I knew that it was the right move for us to make, but my gut was telling me something was off. I felt like a storm was coming, and it was likely to tear us all apart. I feared that once it passed, nothing would ever be the same.

I had no idea how things were going to play out with the Black Diamonds, and I couldn't leave Courtney without telling her exactly how I felt. It'd been two days since I'd seen her at the club, and even with all the shit that was going down, I hadn't been able to get her off my mind. I'd tried to give her the space she needed, but I couldn't stay away any longer. I knew she was fighting it, but after that kiss, she couldn't hide how she felt. I'd been patient and given her time, but I was done waiting. She was mine, and it was time that she remembered that.

It was almost time for Courtney to get off work when I drove into the school parking lot. Maverick was waiting for her when I pulled up next to him.

"Hey, man. Is something up?" Maverick asked.

"Need to take care of some things with Court," I told him.

"Yeah, I figured this was coming. About time for you two to sort this shit out," he said as he got on his bike. "You know, she's not going to make it easy."

"No doubt about that."

"Good luck," Maverick said as he started up his engine.

I nodded and watched as he pulled out of the parking lot. Courtney started walking towards me right as he hit the highway.

"What's going on? Where's he going?" she asked with a confused look.

"I sent him home. We need to get some things settled." She looked at me like I'd lost my damn mind, and I knew she was about to give me a hard time. "Get on the bike, Court. I have something I need to show you."

"Umm, no. I'm not going anywhere with you, Bobby," Courtney said as she crossed her arms.

"Get on the damn bike, Court," I demanded.

"Did you not hear what I just said? I am not going anywhere with you. Besides, it's cold, Bobby, and you have nothing that I want to see right now." I could tell she was about to give in, but I wasn't going to take any chances.

"I'm not going to tell you again. Get on the bike, or I'm going to come over there and put you on it my damn self."

Courtney huffed loudly, but she did as she was told. She walked over to me and placed her hands on my shoulders as she pulled herself onto the seat. I grabbed her school stuff and placed it in my saddlebag.

"Exactly where are we going?" she asked angrily. She was mad, but having her back on my bike was a start.

"Not far," I told her. I knew that if I told her we were going back to my place she would freak out. Besides, she'd find out soon enough.

When we pulled up in my driveway, she started in. "*Really*?" she said in the drawn out sarcastic way she did when she was pissed. "What the hell, Bobby? There's no way I'm going in there. Bringing me here is just a waste of time."

I didn't respond. I got off the bike and started walking towards the front door. I didn't have to look back. I knew that she was sitting on my bike glaring at me with one of her "I'm going to kill you in your sleep" looks. I unlocked the door and walked into the house. I hoped her curiosity would work to my advantage, so I left her sitting there. If there was any part of her that still wanted me, she'd come walking through that front door. Deep down, she knew I wouldn't have brought her here if I didn't have a good reason.

Several minutes passed, and I began to have my doubts. Maybe I was wrong about everything. I ran my hands across the back of my neck and released a deep breath. Fuck. I started walking back out to the bike but stopped suddenly when I found her standing at the front door. Relief instantly washed over me. I couldn't hold back my smile as she walked into the living room and rolled her eyes at me.

"So what is it that you have to show me, Bobby? It's freezing out there," she said with frustration.

I took her hand and led her back to my bedroom. She started to resist, but I pulled her close to me. "Just give me five minutes. After that, if you still want to end things between us, I'll let you go. It will be the hardest fucking thing I've ever had to do, but I won't try to change your mind."

She looked at me, her eyes full of doubt and said, "Okay. You have five minutes." She sat down on the edge of my bed and crossed her arms as she waited to see what I had to show her. I reached behind her for the Christmas gift I'd planned to give her before the accident. A questioning look spread on her face as I placed the gift in her hand.

"Open it," I told her.

She quickly started to tear open the envelope, but she froze when she began to read what was inside. Her eyes roamed over the words, but she didn't say anything. I could tell she was shocked to see the two tickets to Telluride, Colorado, and the hotel reservations for a small log cabin in the mountains.

"You were going to take me there for Christmas break?" she asked.

"You told me you always wanted to learn how to snowboard," I reminded her. Silence filled the room as she thought about what I'd just said.

"You remembered that?" she asked. "I told you that the first day we met at the carnival."

"I remember everything that's important to me, Courtney. You are the most important thing in the world to me, so… yes, I remembered."

She sighed deeply as she held the tickets in her hand. She was deep in thought when I handed her the second box. She stared at it with sadness in her eyes. I could tell that she was having doubts about opening it. She looked up at me and said softly, "I don't see how this changes anything, Bobby."

"Just open the box. Please."

She shook her head as she lifted the top off of the box. Tears began to fill her eyes as she noticed the leather jacket inside. "Why?" she asked as she shook her head from side to side. "Why are you doing this now? It's too late."

"Look at the date on the receipt, baby," I told her, hoping that she'd understand. She reached for the small slip of paper, and her eyes squinted as she searched for the date.

"November 24th? You've had this since November?" she asked in surprise.

"I'd planned to give it to you during Thanksgiving break. I had it all worked out, but everything changed when Renegade claimed Taylor. I didn't want you to have to share that with her."

"You know I wouldn't care about that," she told me.

"I know. I just wanted it to be special. Something you'd always remember. I wanted it to be perfect," I told her as I brushed the hair out of her face.

"I didn't want perfect, Bobby. I wanted you," she said as she looked down at the jacket. Her fingers traced over the embroidery as she said, "I don't know what to do. I'm so confused."

"I love you, Courtney. I've made my mistakes, but you know that I've always loved you. Leaving you that day in the hospital was the hardest thing I've ever had to do," I told her as I took the box out of her hands. I leaned over her to place my mouth close to her ear and whispered, "You know this thing between us isn't over. It will never be over." I felt her body tense as I began to kiss her neck. I leaned forward, urging her to lie back on the bed. Her thighs opened slightly, allowing me to rest between her legs. A low moan vibrated through her chest as I pressed my lips against hers. She didn't resist as I slowly began to remove her shirt. "Tell me," I urged as I ground my growing erection into her center. Her legs instinctively wrapped around me, bringing me closer to her.

"Baby, tell me." I could feel her heart pounding against my chest, but she didn't respond. I slowly began to pull away from her. She reached for my waist, trying to keep me close, but I refused to continue unless she gave me the answer I needed.

CHAPTER 9

COURTNEY

I DIDN'T CARE what had happened in the past. I wanted him. I'd always wanted him, and I was done fighting it.

"It's not over, Bobby," I whispered as my fingers drifted to his neck, tangling in his hair. His mouth collided against mine, intensifying my need for him. I couldn't wait a moment longer. I moved my hands down to undo the buttons of my jeans. I lifted my hips long enough for him to remove them, along with my panties. Like my shirt, they fell useless to the floor.

He pulled his shirt over his head before he leaned back over me. "You're mine, Courtney. You always have been. You just didn't know it." The warmth of his breath caressed my skin as he continued, "Now, I'll make sure you never forget." He lifted himself from me just long enough to remove his jeans and toss them to the floor. I was consumed with desire as he lowered himself back between my legs. My fingers dug into his waist, pulling him closer. A low growl vibrated through his chest as his erection brushed against me.

"Please, Bobby…" I pleaded.

"I know, baby. I can't wait to feel you wrapped around my cock," he said as his fingers tugged at my hair. His kisses trailed along my neck, sending chills throughout my body. I reached between us and enclosed my fingers around his thick shaft. The anticipation of having him inside me was almost too much to bear. I slowly stroked him up and down before positioning him at my entrance, encouraging him to finally give me what I was waiting for.

"I missed you," Bobby whispered as he slowly drove inside me. He made deliberate, shallow thrusts that filled me with anguish and heated my blood. I tried to pull him further inside me, but he wouldn't let me. He knew he was hitting the spot that would make me scream out in pleasure and continued to taunt me. I bit my bottom lip in sweet agony as he rolled his hips into me over and over. His rhythm never faltered as he gently slipped my bra strap down my shoulder. His kisses followed his touch as he pulled my breast free. He gently squeezed it in his hand, and I cried out in pleasure as he tormented my nipple with his mouth. My legs wrapped around his waist, and I rocked my hips against him, trying to pull him deeper. His hands dug into my sides, holding me still, as he thrust faster against my g-spot. I heard my whimper echo through the room. I couldn't catch my breath as I scratched down his back, lost in the rhythm he was building with each push. My body trembled with anticipation.

I could feel my climax building, burning through my

veins. "Bobby, please," I begged, rousing him to fuck me harder.

"Look at me, Courtney," he said as his eyes seared into me. "Is this what you want, baby?"

I opened my eyes and saw the lust in his gaze. He grabbed the headboard in one hand and a fist of my hair in the other and thrust deeply, fully inside me. I cried out as I spread my legs wider, trying to take more of him.

He released the headboard and reached for my leg, lifting my ankle over his shoulder. He pulled back out slowly, almost completely, before he drove deeply back inside me, taking my breath. He continued to thrust as I tightened around his cock. I was panting and gasping for breath, ready to lose control as my muscles began to quiver. He put his hands under my ass, lifting me higher as he angled inside me, finding the spot he knew would send me over the edge.

"Yes!" I cried out as my nails dug into his chest. My eyes clamped shut as my orgasm surged through my body. A loud, torturous groan escaped him as my body shook with violent tremors. I was lost in my own intoxicating pleasure when he finally found his own release. His brows furrowed as he thrust forcefully into me one last time. My leg dropped to his side as he kissed me, before letting his body fall down on the bed beside me.

He rolled to his side and pulled me over to him. My back pressed against his chest, while his arm wrapped around my waist. I laid there silently listening as our erratic breathing slowed into a steady rhythm. Goosebumps rose on my skin as his lips brushed across my shoulder.

"You could have told me," I whispered.

"I almost did, but after seeing you in that hospital, fighting for your life, I just couldn't. I thought you were right to push me away."

"Bobby, the accident wasn't your fault. You can't blame yourself for what happened."

"You'll never know what seeing you like that did to me. I'll never let anything happen to you again, baby, and I'm going to make those motherfuckers pay for what they did," he promised.

I turned to my side so I could face him. He had such determination in his eyes that it scared me. "No, Bobby. Please just leave them alone. I don't know what I would do if something happened to you. It's just not worth it!" I cried.

"You're worth it, Courtney. They went after you and my club. I can't let them get away with this shit. This is something I *have* to do."

"What are you going to do?" I asked.

"You know I can't tell you about it," he said as he leaned over and lightly kissed my temple. His fingers trailed over my bare skin as his eyes roamed my body.

"When? Can you at least tell me when this is going to happen?" I asked, lifting myself up on my elbows and ignoring his attempt to distract me.

"Tomorrow," he said as he began nipping at my neck. He cupped my breast in his hand, and slowly brushed his thumb over my nipple.

"What are you doing?" I asked. A devilish grin spread across his face.

"Making up for lost time," he said, pulling me over on top of him. "I can't get enough of you." My knees fell to his sides as they straddled his waist. His hands dropped to my hips, gliding me over his erection. His fingers dug into my thighs as I took him in my hand and slid him inside me. My head tossed back as I slowly slid up and down his cock. I reached for his shoulders as I continued to ride him with everything I had. When our eyes met, I was overcome with emotion. I loved him so much. He was going to put his life in danger because of me, and there was nothing I could do to stop him. I fought back my tears as my hips rolled back and forth, taking him deeper with each move. I wanted to cling to him, to keep him close so I knew he'd be safe, but I knew it was impossible.

We spent the rest of the night wrapped in each other's arms and making love. We never even left the bed. I felt whole for the first time since the accident. Being with him made me feel safe, and I dreaded the thought of him leaving. I had no idea what his plans were, but I could tell that it was weighing on his mind. I didn't push him to talk about it, because I already knew that he couldn't tell me. I just did the only thing I could do; I made our night together one that he would always remember.

CHAPTER 10

The man that seeks revenge
digs two graves.
Ken Kesey

BOBBY

———⟡◉◉◉⟡———

"WHAT TIME IS it?" Courtney asked frantically. I rolled over to check the time on my phone, and I knew she was going to freak out when I told her. "It's 7:15."

"Damn it! I'm going to be late," she screeched as she jumped out of bed and raced to the bathroom. As she turned on the shower, she yelled, "I don't have anything to wear to work!"

"I got you clothes to wear." I'd bought her clothes for today, in hopes that she'd come back to me. I wanted to make sure she'd have what she needed if she stayed. I didn't want her to have any regrets. She needed to know that I'd make sure she was taken care of.

"I can't believe I'm this late!" she shouted as she stepped into the shower. I got up, grabbed her new clothes, and laid them on the bed. She had several things that she'd left in one of my spare drawers, so I knew she wouldn't have any problem putting something together. I got dressed and went into the kitchen to make her some coffee.

I was pouring her a cup when she ran in and said, "I gotta go." Her hair was still wet and she wasn't wearing any makeup, but damn she looked good in that outfit.

"Looking good, babe," I said, wrapping my arm around her waist.

"Thanks for the clothes, Bobby. They're perfect," she said as she pulled her hair up into one of those messy bun things. She leaned over and kissed me quickly on the lips before she said, "Seriously, I gotta get to work."

I hated the thought of her leaving, knowing that I would already be gone when she got off work. I pulled her close to me and said, "I want you to be extra careful while I'm gone. Listen to Maverick and try not to give him a hard time."

She froze in my arms as my words washed over her. Her lips trembled as she said, "I don't want you to go." Her eyes pleaded with me to stay. She shook her head and said, "I get that you have to do this…. All I ask is that you come back to me."

"I'll be back. You can count on that," I told her. I pulled her close to me, holding her tight against my chest. I wanted to say more, but I didn't have time. "Let's get you to work." I kissed her one last time before leading her outside.

It was hard to watch her get off my bike and walk

into that school, but I felt better knowing that she'd be waiting for me when I got back. I was ready to get the shit with the Black Diamonds sorted out. I still had my doubts about how it was all going to play out, but I decided it was just my nerves. I'd always been the man behind the scenes, but this was my chance to be on the front lines of all the action. I needed to shake off my doubts and prepare for what lay ahead.

CHAPTER 11

COURTNEY

———————◦◦◦◦———————

I MADE IT to my classroom just as the bell was ringing. The kids started streaming into the room just like it was any other day. I was thankful that they were all oblivious to my frazzled state of mind. I was putting their morning assignment up on the board when Tessa stopped at my door. As soon as I saw the huge smile on her face, I knew that she was going to give me a hard time.

She cleared her throat exaggeratedly. "Can I talk to you for a minute?" she asked as she crossed her arms and propped her back against the doorframe.

"Umm... Ms. Campbell, right now isn't a *good time*," I told her sternly.

"It will only take a minute," she said with a wide smile.

"Give me just a second," I told her as I finished writing the assignment on the board. I turned to the students and said, "Class, this assignment needs to be completed in your journal. Write at least two para-graphs." As I walked towards Tessa, I added, "Thomas, take names. I will be just outside in the hall with Ms. Campbell." I stepped outside and readied myself for her scrutiny.

"You look *nice* today. That's a really cute skirt," Tessa said as her eyes roamed over my new outfit. I really liked it, too. The gray pencil skirt had a slight flare at the bottom, which really flattered my figure. It looked great with the purple V-neck sweater Bobby had bought to go with it. It had a professional look, but wearing it made me feel sexy.

"Thanks. Did you need something, or did you just want to compliment my clothes?" I asked her sarcastically.

"Oh, no, it's nothing really. Just checking on you. You were running late this morning, and I just wanted to make sure everything was okay," she said sincerely.

"Everything is fine, Tessa," I replied. "Just overslept."

"Mm-hmm?" she asked, egging me on.

"Yes. Now, I have to get back to my class before one of the boys decides to have a spitball fight. I hate having those nasty little things stuck to my ceiling," I told her.

Her hands shot to her hips. "So, you're really not going to tell me what happened with Bobby last night?" she asked disapprovingly.

"*Why* are you asking if you already know?" I asked as I crossed my arms.

"I don't know the details," she said excitedly. "I want details!"

"I don't have time for *details* right now, Tess. You'll

have to come back at lunch, and I will fill you in on everything," I told her.

She sighed and said, "Okay, but I want to hear everything." She added in a whisper, "No leaving out the good parts!"

"How do you know there are good parts? It could've all been bad... very, very bad," I told her with a devious smile.

"I knew the minute I saw you this morning that it was good. I haven't seen you smile like that in weeks!" she laughed.

"Lunch," I told her as I headed back into my classroom. The students were actually doing what I told them to do, which was a pleasant surprise. They'd all been on their best behavior since I'd come back after the accident. Thankfully, they remained quiet all morning as they completed their work.

Tessa was waiting at my door as soon as the lunch bell rang. I shook my head as she walked into my room.

"Impatient much?" I asked.

"Spill it," she said as she walked over to my back table and unpacked her lunch. "I want to hear every detail."

I spent the next twenty minutes telling her everything that had happened with Bobby, and by the time I was finished the lunch period was almost over.

"So, he gave you the jacket. I can't wait to see it!" she said.

"I can't believe I left it at his house. Getting his jacket was all I thought about for so long, and I didn't even have a chance to try it on. We were so distracted last night, I totally forgot about it," I told her.

"Don't worry about it. You can show me later," she replied. "I really do think it was sweet that he wanted to wait until it was the perfect time."

"I just wish he'd told me. I spent so much time thinking that he didn't want me, and it really hurt," I told her.

"I know, honey, but Bobby has always been crazy about you. That's the only thing that ever really mattered," she said as she squeezed my hand.

"I know that now. I guess I just needed time to figure it all out," I told her just as the bell rang.

"I'll call you tonight," Tessa said. I nodded as she headed for the door. Before the class got back to the room, I grabbed my phone and sent Bobby a text.

Me: *I miss you already*

Bobby: *I won't be gone long*

Me: *I love my new outfit*

Bobby: *You looked damn hot in that skirt*

Me: *Wanna know a secret?*

Bobby: *???*

Me: *Wearing this skirt reminds me of that night at the bar. Remember?*

Bobby: *How could I forget?*

I couldn't suppress the smile that spread across my face as I thought back to that night.

We'd been drinking at the bar, and everyone had left to go home except us. All the lights were off, except the one over the bar. Bobby took my hand and led me over to the darkened corner behind the pool tables. I looked at him questioningly as he pulled me up against him. He put one of his hands behind my neck as he pressed his mouth against mine. My lips parted in surprise as he backed me against the wall. His tongue swept across my open lips before dipping seductively into my mouth.

His hands gripped my ass as he pressed his hips against mine. I could feel his arousal even through his jeans. His hands roamed restlessly over my body as his mouth moved to my neck. His kisses were urgent, and I was quickly becoming lost in the heat of his need.

"Bobby... Bobby... wait... what if somebody sees us?" I asked.

"Camera blind spot... door's locked," he murmured between kisses. His hand greedily moved under my shirt, caressing my breast over my bra.

"You're sure? What if someone comes back in? The guys have keys...." I protested as he raised his head to look at me.

The fiery lust that filled his eyes stopped my words. I could tell in that moment that nothing would stop him. I had seen that look before. When Bobby needed me, nothing else existed. Nothing else could satisfy him.

The hunger in his eyes made me want to please him. I let my inhibitions fall away as my desire for him took over. In that moment, I needed him every bit as much as he needed me. I needed to see his chiseled body, to feel his mouth on me. I needed him inside of me, making me come undone. I tore at his button-down and watched with satisfaction as it ripped open, the buttons scattering on the floor. He shrugged the shirt off and grinned devilishly as I bit my lip and lifted my arms over my head.

His hands slid up my body, taking my shirt with them and dropping it to the floor. His fingers slid inside the cups of my bra, pulling my breasts free. I licked my lips in anticipation as he leaned back, his eyes devouring me. A low growl rumbled in his throat as his hands ran up my back and unhooked my bra. My fingers gripped his shoulders as his head lowered to my nipple. His tongue flicked across the tip before his lips surrounded it and began sucking with gentle pressure. I began to pant as he moved to my other breast, and a shiver ran over me as the cold air hit my nipple where his mouth had been.

Bobby took a step back as he grabbed my waist and turned me to face the wall. I dropped my bra to the floor as I felt him gently sweep my hair over my shoulder and brush his lips across the nape of my neck.

"Put your hands on the wall," he commanded.

A rush surged through my body as I placed my palms on the cool plaster and waited for him to continue. I felt the intense heat of his body radiating against my naked back as he placed his hands on my outer thighs. A small moan escaped me as his rough fingertips began to slide my skirt upwards. His thumbs hooked in the waist of my lace panties as he dragged them slowly down to my ankles. As I stepped out of them, I felt his fingertips trail up the inside of my thighs. My breath caught as he slid his middle finger along my center, testing me. "Mmm, wet for me already?"

I heard him unfasten his jeans as he continued tormenting me. Suddenly, I felt his thick erection slide between my legs as one of his hands grabbed my hip. He reached between us and positioned himself at my entrance before thrusting inside of me in one hard, *smooth stroke.*

A hiss escaped his lips as my body squeezed around him, adjusting to the fullness. I moaned in pleasure, relishing the feeling of him buried inside of me. His hands reached up to cup my breasts as he began shallow thrusts, readying me. He rolled his hips in anguishing rhythm as my fingers grasped at the wall in desperation. His hands moved down to still my hips as he began driving into me with longer, deeper strokes. My body trembled and my breathing became ragged as my climax approached. I gasped as one of his hands reached around to tease my clit. The gentle pressure of his finger overwhelmed me and sent me over the edge.

"Oh, God! Bobby!" I cried as the waves of ecstasy rolled through my body. The pleasure was so intense, my legs momentarily buckled. His strong hands gripped my hips and held me upright as my body contracted around his hard cock. My muscles struggled to push him out, but his thrusts were relentless as he quickened his pace, chasing his own release. I began to rock my hips back into his, wanting him to be as satisfied as I was. I felt his cock swell inside me as he reached his orgasm. His growl echoed in the room as his rhythm slowed.

I quickly pulled myself back to the present as my students came walking into the room. I smiled as I looked down at my phone, reading the message he'd sent again. *How could I forget?* I felt exactly the same way.

CHAPTER 12

War must be, while we defend our lives against a destroyer who would devour all; but I do not love the bright sword for its sharpness, nor the arrow for its swiftness, nor the warrior for his glory. I love only that for which they defend.

J. R. R. Tolkien

BOBBY

SHEPPARD, RENEGADE, AND Goliath were talking with Bishop when I walked into the clubhouse. They were studying the map he had spread out on the table. He was looking for the best location for us to lay low while we waited for the Black Diamonds. After a heated discussion, we all finally agreed on two possible locations. We wouldn't know which for sure until we got there. Once we arrived, we could decide which place provided us with the best coverage. Bishop called Snake to finalize the plan.

Once they agreed on all the details, we followed Goliath to the back of the garage. He'd been meticulously going over the entire weapon inventory, making sure everyone was prepared. He unlocked the gun safe and gave us each several handguns and several boxes of ammo. We could've killed a fucking army with everything he'd given us. I took the gun in my hand as anxiety rushed through my veins. I'd never killed a man before, but there was a good chance that was about to change. I slipped the gun in the back holster Goliath had given me and placed the other gun in my shoulder harness.

"We need to get going," Goliath announced as he continued to conceal his weapons. "I want to have a chance to look around before the drop off."

"How many men are they supposed to have picking up the delivery?" Sheppard asked.

"Four guys are dropping off, and two guys are picking up," Goliath responded. "It should be a routine drop."

Goliath continued to load a large duffle bag full of rifles and handguns. He wanted to be prepared for anything, but I really hoped we wouldn't need them.

"Just keep your eyes open. Snake's men are prepared to take these guys out, but that's not what we're there for. Our focus is getting that shipment. Get in. Get out," Goliath said firmly.

"Let's get this party started," Sheppard said, smiling. He'd seen plenty of shit during his time in the army, so he wasn't even fazed by what was happening. I wished I felt the same way.

The Black Diamonds were scheduled to arrive at the abandoned gas station at 6:30. By the time we got there, we only had forty-five minutes to decide which location was best and get into our positions. Snake's Sergeant of Arms, Bones, had his men set up behind the old garage. It would have good visuals, since it was connected to the gas station. I thought it was too risky, but they intended to make their move as soon as they started unloading the crates.

We opted to take cover in an abandoned barn across the street. Goliath kept watch while Renegade and I pulled the truck around back. We were still getting everything out of the truck when the first SUV pulled into the lot. I watched as the doors flew open, and four men stepped out of the truck. Once we'd made it inside the barn, I was able to get a better view. I immediately noticed that those men didn't resemble typical bikers. They looked more like kids that would've played on the high school football team. I didn't understand it. They were just fucking kids. What the hell were they doing there? We watched as they goofed around, haphazardly scanning the area. Even though they were far from threatening, I was relieved when they didn't seem to detect us.

"What the fuck are they doing?" Renegade asked as he watched behind me. "This has to be some kind of fucking joke, man."

He stopped talking as soon as an old, beat-up Ford Explorer started pulling into the lot. We watched silently as two of the boys casually walked over to the driver's side and started talking. They stood there, nodding and talking, completely unaware that we were watching them. We were waiting for them to start unloading the truck, when I felt the hair on the back of my neck rise.

In the distance, I heard the faint rumble of motorcycles coming in our direction. As the roar of the engines got closer, one of the kids looked over in our direction and smiled. Smiled! Goddamn it! They knew we were there.

"It's a fucking ambush," Sheppard shouted.

Everything was a blur as we drew our weapons and tried to prepare for the onslaught. We watched as the four guys raced back into their SUV and started the engine. Snake's men began shooting at them, but they made it out unscathed. We didn't have time to chase them, because a parade of bikers came driving by with their weapons drawn. Pieces of wood and debris exploded around us as bullets tore through the old barn walls. Without hesitation, we all returned fire, but the flying fragments of wood made it difficult to see. We quickly realized that our handguns were no match for their high power semi-automatic rifles.

"Pull back!" Goliath shouted. A searing pain slashed through my arm as I continued to shoot, determined to reach my target. I watched with satisfaction as his body dropped to the ground, his bike crashing. Gunfire continued to explode around us, filling the barn with dust and blurring my vision. Renegade grabbed my jacket and pulled me towards the back of the barn. We both ducked down as the bullets continued to assault us. Sheppard refused to leave his post, though, shooting at anything and everything in his line of vision. Goliath grunted angrily as he reached over to grab Sheppard's arm and pull him away from the window.

Suddenly the gunfire stopped, leaving us surrounded by silence. Goliath stood and carefully walked over to one of the side windows. After scanning the area, he said, "They're gone."

"What the fuck was that?" Renegade demanded. "Goddamn it! How did they know we were here?"

"That's a good fucking question," Goliath growled as he stormed out of the barn. The air felt thick as we followed him over to the back of the garage. Bile rose in my throat as we walked past the dead bodies lying mangled on the road. It was difficult to look at all the carnage, especially since I knew it was far from over. I knew there would be more gunfire, more bloodshed, and more death.

Once we made it behind the garage, the scene before me only got worse. Two of the Red Dragons had been fatally shot, but Bones continued to try and save them. They had both suffered bullet wounds to the head that left no chance for their survival. Anger flashed through Bones' face as he realized he couldn't help them.

"Goddamn it!" Bones shouted.

"They're gone, man. It's over," Goliath said. Bones stood up, covered in his brother's blood, and slammed his fist into the side of the garage. His face showed a mixture of fury and pain as he looked down on the fallen members of his club.

"They knew we were coming," he snarled at Goliath. "How the fuck did they know we'd be here?"

"That's what we wanna know," Goliath snapped.

"Got no idea, but I intend to find out," he grunted. Bones reached for his phone and started to text Snake.

"I need to call Bishop," Goliath said as he turned to face us. He grimaced as he saw my arm.

"Sheppard, see how bad it is," Goliath said, nodding towards me. In the mayhem that had just transpired, I'd totally forgotten about being shot. Sheppard gently ripped the sleeve of my shirt, exposing my bullet wound. He lifted my elbow, and I cringed as the pain ripped through my arm.

"Looks like it went straight through," he said as he continued to examine me. "But we're gonna need someone to look at it. It's bleeding like a bitch."

"He's lost a lot of blood. We'll take him back to our clubhouse. It's closer, and Mac can stitch him up," Bones offered.

Renegade turned to me and said, "I don't know if that's a good idea."

"I'll go, just let me get my bag," I told them. I turned back to Renegade and asked, "Mind giving me a hand?"

He nodded and followed me back to the truck. "You sure about this?" he asked with concern.

"The Black Diamonds knew we'd be here waiting for them today. There has to be something that we're missing here, Renegade. Maybe I can find out what it is," I replied.

"Watch your back, Crack Nut," he told me as he grabbed my bag from his truck. "Right now, we don't know who we can trust."

CHAPTER 13

COURTNEY

━━━━◦◦◦◦◦━━━━

Y OU KNOW THAT feeling you get in the pit of your stomach when you know something is wrong, but you just can't figure out what it is. It's like something you've done is about to catch up with you, and you know that it isn't going to be good. I'd had that feeling all freaking day, and it was about to drive me out of my mind.

At first I'd thought it had something to do with school—maybe a mad parent, or an evaluation that didn't go very well, but that wasn't it. Even long after the school day had ended, that gnawing feeling continued to worry me. I just couldn't put my finger on what was wrong.

When I got home from work, Maverick didn't make it any better. He was all "Mr. Serious" and wouldn't even talk to me. It was obvious that something was bothering him, but as usual, I had no idea what it was. I could only assume that it had to do with the club. You would've thought they'd have been able to tell me something. I hated being left out of the loop. There was nothing I could do to change it, though, so I had to let it go. Hopefully whatever was bothering him would pass soon, and things would get back to normal. I would have to just try and be patient.

It was getting late, and the tension in the house was growing by the minute. I needed to get my mind off of things for a bit, so I decided to check in with my mother. That was a huge mistake. Our conversation had been going fine, until I mentioned that Bobby and I were back together. To say the least, she wasn't happy. After a ten-minute lecture on "needing to do what was best for me", I made an excuse to get off the phone. Deep down, I knew she just wanted me to be happy, but she was wasting her breath. Nothing she could've said was going to change my mind about being with Bobby.

When the phone call didn't work out, I tried to keep myself busy by cleaning the house. As I made my way back to my bedroom, I was surprised to see a familiar box lying on the bed. I walked over to read the note that was resting on top.

You're mine, baby.
Then. Now. Always.
Bobby

I smiled as I read the card again. I considered trying it on to see how I looked in it, but I wanted to wait until Bobby was there with me. I wanted to share that moment with him, so I put the box away and hoped that I could try it on for him soon. I prayed that I wouldn't have to wait long to show him. I began to wonder if he was my source of worry. My stomach was still tied into knots, and I knew something had to be wrong.

I fixed a nice dinner for Maverick and me, but neither of us had much of an appetite. We were lost in our own thoughts and barely said a word to each other. As we were putting our dishes away, Maverick's phone rang. He grabbed it and headed into the living room.

His voice was too low for me to hear what he was saying, so I silently eased my way into the room with him.

"How the fuck did they know?" he whispered. There was a long pause before he continued, "Was anybody hurt?"

I could hear the concern in his voice, and it made my heart race with worry. His question replayed over and over in my head. *Was anybody hurt?* I knew in my heart that that was the moment that had been haunting me all day. Deep down, I'd known it was coming.

"Why are they taking him there?" he asked. He looked anxious as he paced back and forth across the living room floor. "What do you need me to do?" He stopped and turned in my direction. He didn't look happy to see me standing there listening to him, but he continued talking. "You got it. Call me if you need me." He hung up the phone and dropped it on the sofa.

"What did they say? Was it about Bobby? Is he okay?" I asked frantically.

He ran his fingers through his hair, trying to find the right words to say to me. I felt like my heart actually stopped beating as I waited for him to say *something*. I held my breath, at once dreading the news but needing it all the same.

"Things didn't go so well tonight."

"And?" I asked, feeling the pressure building in my chest. Every breath I took was pure agony. I was consumed with doubt and worry as I waited for him to explain.

"The less you know the better, Courtney, but Bobby is going to be okay. I really can't tell you more than that."

"Going to be okay? What the hell does that mean?" I asked angrily. It infuriated me that he wasn't willing to give me any more than that. I didn't give him a chance to respond before I said, "Maverick, you have to tell me what's going on with Bobby! You can't seriously expect…."

"He was shot, Courtney. It was a clean shot to the arm, and they said he's going to be fine. They're taking him back to Snake's clubhouse, so they can check him out," Maverick confessed.

"He was shot?! I can't believe you weren't going to tell me that!" I screamed. "And why isn't he coming home? Why would they take him to *Snake's* clubhouse? That doesn't make any fucking sense!"

"Getting upset isn't going to help anything, Courtney. Snake's place was closer. It was the right thing to do. He'll call you when he can, but it's going to be a while. For now, you've got to be patient."

"How the hell am I supposed to be patient?" I said

as the tears began to stream down my face. I felt so helpless. I wanted to see Bobby and make sure he was okay. I couldn't even talk to him. I threw my hands in the air and said, "I don't think I can handle this!"

Maverick walked over to me and calmly said, "You *can* handle it. You've gotten through worse things than this. Everything will work out. Just give it time."

"How much time, Maverick? Just tell me how long he's going to be gone," I pleaded.

"I really don't know," he said as he walked over to me. He rested his hands on my shoulders and said, "Sometimes we just have to live on faith, Courtney. You have to believe in Bobby the way he believes in you."

I let out a deep sigh, and without saying another word, I turned away from him. I needed to be alone, so I could pull myself together. I went to my bedroom and searched for the t-shirt Bobby had left there a few weeks ago. When I finally found it, I slipped it on and grabbed my new jacket. I laid it across my lap and brushed my fingers across the embroidery, wishing that Bobby were there with me. I laid it on the bed beside me and got under the covers. I pulled his fleece blanket tight around me. I wanted to be strong, but thinking of Bobby being hurt was more than I could stand. My brain was tormented with thoughts of him being in pain as I tossed and turned in the bed. I couldn't fight back the tears. There was no use even trying. I pulled my knees up to my chest and finally let the tears fall freely, crying myself to sleep.

CHAPTER 14

It is during our darkest moments that
we must focus to see the light.

Aristotle Onassis

BOBBY

W HEN WE PULLED into the Red Dragon's compound, it didn't look like the same place. They'd
made several advancements in their security system, and
they'd added more guards to the front gate. I had no
doubt that our club had something to do with their
changes. It was obvious that they weren't happy about us
breaking into their clubhouse, and they had no intention
of letting that happen again.

By the time we walked into the clubhouse, the adren-
aline racing through my veins had completely worn off.
My shirt was totally soaked in blood, and my arm was
killing me. Bones helped me down the long hallway to
Mac's room. Apparently, he was the medic for their club,
but he looked more like a serial killer to me. It took him
over an hour to stitch up my arm. He told me I was
lucky that the bullet didn't cause more damage than it

did. It fractured part of the bone in my arm on its way out, and he warned me that it might cause a problem. He was more concerned about infection. He gave me a shot of strong antibiotics and painkillers before sending me to one of the spare rooms to rest.

It was after midnight before I was finally able to shake off the daze of the medication. The place was quiet so I assumed that everyone had decided to call it a night. It'd been a long day, and it had taken its toll on all of us. I eased myself out of the bed and looked around the room. I was surprised to see how much it resembled our rooms back at home. There was a bed and a flat screen TV, but that room also had a large desk with a laptop computer.

I wasn't going to be able to go back to sleep with my arm hurting like it was, so I figured it might be a good time to do a little research. I sat down at the desk to turn on the computer. The first thing I noticed was that the green webcam light was on. It could've been nothing, but it made me wonder if someone was watching. I did my best to log into the computer without drawing attention to the fact that I knew the webcam was on.

It didn't take me long to figure out that it was Cage's old computer. He was Taylor's ex-boyfriend, and he'd caused all kinds of problems. His road name was Tank, and at one time he was Snake's Sergeant of Arms. That had all ended when we discovered his plans to take over the Red Dragons. Snake wasn't expecting to hear that one of his own wanted him dead. He'd killed Cage, and no one blamed him for it. No one would've expected anything less from a president like Snake. He was a strong leader, willing to do anything for his club.

After a few minutes of searching the hard drive, I realized that their anti-malware was out of date. There was nothing protecting their system, and anyone could've easily hacked into it. I continued digging and quickly found out that the Black Diamonds had gotten into Snake's server. They were able to get into the system using a virus they'd sent to Cage's email from a man named Justin Taylor. His club name was Razor, and he was the Black Diamond's VP. Once Cage opened the email, it corrupted his entire system. Dummy emails were sent to each member of Snake's club, spreading the virus everywhere. That gave the Black Diamonds full access to everything on their server, including the webcams. They'd pulled the classic Trojan horse.

I had to admit, it was a pretty fucking smart move. By using the webcams, they were able to watch every-thing that was happening in the club, and the Red Dragons didn't suspect a thing. Fuck! That's how they knew we were going to be there waiting for them. I logged off the computer without removing any of the spyware that had been used to corrupt the system. I hoped we might be able to use it to our advantage. I decided it was time to pull our own fucking Trojan horse.

CHAPTER 15

COURTNEY

"I'VE GOTTA GET back to Washington," Maverick said as he closed his laptop.

"Is everything okay?" I asked.

A remorseful look crossed his face as he said, "I shouldn't have left. I don't know why I let them talk me into this."

"I don't know why you had to leave, Maverick, but I know you wouldn't have left unless it was something you had to do," I told him.

"I should be there helping them sort this shit out, not babysitting some girl from another fucking club," he said angrily.

"Wow, why don't you tell me how you really feel," I said, placing my hands on my hips. I wasn't really angry with him, but his words still hurt. I knew he was only saying that because he was upset.

"Fuck. I didn't mean that, Courtney. This has nothing to do with you," he said quietly. "Actually, being with you has been the only thing that kept me sane over the past few weeks."

"Are you sure that you have to go back?" I asked.

"I should've gone back weeks ago. I just hope it isn't too late," he said as he put his laptop in his duffle bag. "You need to get some stuff together. I've gotta take you over to the clubhouse."

"What? Why?" I asked.

"The club is still under lockdown, and Bishop doesn't want you left alone. He wants you to stay in Bobby's room until this blows over."

"Have you heard anything from him yet?" I asked.

"No, but I'm sure he'll call you as soon as he can. Now, go get some things together. I need to get going," he said as he waved his hand, motioning me out of the room.

I shoved as much as I could into two small bags and headed back into the living room. Maverick was already there, packed and waiting for me. "You ready, Cheeks?" he asked. Damn, I was actually going to miss having him around.

"Ready. But... Maverick?"

"Yeah?" he asked.

"I want to thank you for everything you've done over the past few weeks. It meant a lot to me that you were here. You always made me feel safe, and I will never forget that. Please take care of yourself when you get back home," I told him.

"You don't have to thank me, Courtney. I really did enjoy being here with you," he said with a big smile. "You're one in a million, Cheeks."

"Oh stop, before I get all sentimental and crap. Let's

get outta here so you can say goodbye to John Warren before you go."

"I'd like that. It's going to be hard to leave him again, but I'll be back," he said as he grabbed my bags and headed for the door. I really did hate to see him go. I just prayed that whatever was waiting for him back in Washington wouldn't cause him too much trouble.

Once we got to the clubhouse, I went straight to Bobby's room. I wanted to give Maverick some time alone with John Warren. I'd just finished putting my stuff in Bobby's closet when Tessa walked in.

"Hey there, stranger!" she said excitedly. She walked over to me and gave me a big hug. "I was so excited when Bishop said you were coming today."

"I wish I could say the same. I'm new to all this lockdown business. Not sure how I feel about being forced to stay here, Tessa."

"Oh, Courtney. Don't be a Negative Nancy. It'll be fun. It's been so long since we've had a chance to catch up. Now we'll have plenty of time." I didn't know how she did it. She always knew how to put a positive spin on everything.

I wondered if she'd heard anything about Bobby. "Did Bishop say how Bobby was doing?"

"He hasn't said much. He did mention that Bobby was feeling better, and that he was working on something for the club."

"I wish I knew more about what was going on, Tessa. How do you stand not knowing?" I asked.

"I trust Bishop. I know he'll take care of the kids and

me. That's all I really need to know," she said, sounding all calm and rational, but it didn't make me feel one damn bit better.

"I wish I felt that way. I guess I'm just too damn curious. It's like watching only parts of a scary movie and never really getting the plot."

"Scary movies don't have a plot, Courtney. That's the whole point," Tessa said, laughing. "They're nothing like the real world."

"I beg to differ, but we'll hash that out another day. Tell me what's been going on here. How are the kids? Is Myles doing better?" I asked.

"They're fine, just a little cranky at times. They seem to think this is one big bunking party, so they stay up later than they should. I told Bishop we need to add more rooms to this place."

"Izzie can stay in here with me until Bobby gets back if that would help."

"Thanks, sweetie. I may take you up on that." Our attention was drawn over to my purse when my phone beeped with a text message. "Maybe that's Bobby," Tessa said hopefully.

I quickly searched the bottomless pit of my purse for my phone, and my heart raced as I pulled it out. I looked down and relief washed over me as I saw his name on the screen. "It's him!"

"I'll leave you to it. Come find me later, and we'll make up a batch of your famous cookies for the kids."

I nodded and watched her walk out of the room. I sat on his bed and opened the message:

Bobby: Hey baby. You doing okay?

Me: I'm fine. What about you? How's your arm? I've been worried to death about you.

Bobby: It was nothing. I'm fine. You at the club?

Me: In your room right now. Wish you were here with me.

Bobby: I'll be there before you know it.

Me: How much longer are you going to be?

Bobby: Not much longer. Still working through some stuff out here, but I'll be back soon.

Me: Promise?

Bobby: I'd be there right now if I could. I'll be back as soon as I can. Promise.

Me: Good. I miss you.

Bobby: I miss you too, baby.

Me: Are you sure you're okay? Should I be worried?

Bobby: I'm fine. This will all be over before you know it.

Me: I hope so. Take care of yourself.

Bobby: Always. You do the same. I've gotta go. I'll text you again when I can.

I really hated this. I totally sucked at being patient, but I didn't have a choice. There was nothing I could do but wait it out. I just hoped Bobby knew what he was doing, and he would get home soon.

CHAPTER 16

Revenge is but a small circle.
Edward Counsel, Maxims

BOBBY

I DREADED IT, but it was time to break the news to Snake. I didn't want to take any chances on the Black Diamonds using the webcams to hear what I had to say, so I asked him to meet me outside. He had a suspicious look on his face as he followed me out into the parking lot. I took my time explaining what I'd done.

As expected, he was pissed when I told him that I'd spent the entire night searching through their database. After I explained everything to him, his anger was no longer directed at me. At that moment, he was only concerned with finding out what the Black Diamonds were up to and making them pay for what they'd done. He actually asked me to keep looking. He wanted me to find something that he could use to sort the mess out.

After getting the go ahead from Bishop, I went back to Cage's old room and got to work. It took two days to gather all the information that Snake had asked for. In order to recover Cage's full history, I had to do a complete system restore on his laptop. I knew in my gut that it would all lead back to him; there was no other explanation. After a few hours of digging, I finally found what I was looking for. I discovered a flood of emails between Cage and the Black Diamonds. His plan to take Snake out was more involved than we'd originally thought.

I called Snake back outside to tell him what I'd found. "It looks like your man Cage had big plans for your club after he took over," I told him.

"That little cocksucker! What kind of plans was he making?" he asked. The veins in his neck pulsed with anger. I smiled to myself, thinking Cage must have had balls of steel, because Snake wasn't the kind of man you fucked with and expected to get away with it. He was not going to like what I had to tell him about his old Sergeant of Arms, but he needed to hear it.

"Over a year ago, he started communicating with the Black Diamonds. They contacted him with their plans to use the Tennessee River to distribute their weapons. They wanted access to several states, and they thought they had the perfect plan."

"Yeah. We already knew they were trying to use the river. I just don't understand why they went to Cage. Why didn't they just go through me?" Snake asked.

"Cage was a Davenport. His father's company charters sixty percent of the barges running up and down that waterway, from Kentucky all the way down to Alabama. They knew they needed him on board to make their plan work."

"Fuck!" he said angrily. "I gotta say, it was a good plan. A good fucking plan. With me outta the way, Cage would have full control of the club and our distribution." He clenched his fists at his sides as he began to pace in front of me.

"You got it. They weren't happy when Cage stopped communicating with them," I told him. "They tried to contact him several times, but I'm sure they know he's dead by now."

"Best thing I ever did was putting a bullet in that boy's head. Should've done it a long fucking time ago."

"You know, the Black Diamonds are more determined than ever to make this distribution thing happen. It's up to us to stop them," I told him.

"No, it's up to *me* to stop them, and I will. You don't have to worry about that," Snake said firmly.

I gave him a minute to collect his thoughts before I said, "I think you can use those webcams to your advantage. I'd say it's time to take the upper hand."

Snake reached into his back pocket and grabbed his pack of cigarettes. After he took a long hit, he asked, "What do you have in mind?"

"Let's draw them out. Have a little ambush of our own," I told him.

He nodded with a devious smile. "I like your way of thinking, brother," he said as he continued to smoke his cigarette. "I know exactly how to draw those motherfuckers out. Like bees to fucking honey." He reached out to shake my hand. "Bishop's lucky to have you. If you ever need anything, you know who to call."

"Thanks, Snake. I appreciate that," I told him as I took his hand in mine. "Now that we have that sorted, it's time for me to get home."

"I'll have Bones take you back. I'll give Bishop a call and let him know you're on your way."

I went back to my room to grab my bag and met Bones out front. I was anxious to get home. It would be after midnight by the time I got there, but knowing Courtney would be there in my bed made me impatient. I didn't want to waste any time getting back to her.

CHAPTER 17

COURTNEY

"SHE'S MORE THAN welcome to stay in here, Tessa. There's plenty of room, and I'd like to have the company," I explained.

"Ah… well, she's been fighting a fever the last couple of days, and I'm afraid she might have a cold. I don't want you to catch it," Tessa said nervously.

"You didn't mention that she had a fever earlier. What's going on? There's something you're not telling me," I told her. I could tell from the expression on her face that she was hiding something from me.

"Do you always have to think the worst?" she said flippantly. "She has a cold. I don't want you to catch it. *End of story.* Izzie can stay with you another night."

"Whatever, Tessa. It's not like I don't know when you're trying to keep something from me, but I'll let it go this time. Just holler if you change your mind."

"Thanks, Court. Get some rest. You've had a long day," Tessa said as she quickly walked towards the door.

"Okay, boss lady. Whatever you say," I told her sarcastically. I'd figure out what she was hiding later. I was too tired to argue with her right then. I wanted to feel closer to Bobby, so I grabbed one of his oversized t-shirts from his drawer. I tossed my bra over the chair before I slipped it over my head.

I crawled into his bed, and Bobby's scent surrounded me as I pulled the covers over me. God, I missed him. I couldn't wait for him to get back home. Every time I closed my eyes, I saw him staring back at me. I tossed and turned for hours before I was finally able to fall asleep.

I was startled awake when I felt the bed dip down beside me. I quickly turned and found Bobby lying there. I couldn't believe that he was really home. I reached over and ran my hand across his face, needing to be sure that it was really him.

A smile spread across his face as he said, "Hey, baby."

"You came back," I whispered.

"Nothing could keep me away from you," he whispered as he leaned over and pressed his lips against mine. I wrapped my hands around his neck, pulling him closer to me. He slowly lifted himself on top of me, pressing his body against mine. I'd missed the warmth of him more than I'd realized. Without thinking, I reached for the hem of his shirt and tried to pull it over his head. He winced in pain when the shirtsleeve tugged at his arm.

"Oh, God! Your arm... I'm sorry. I didn't...." I started, but he didn't let me continue. Instead, his mouth crashed against mine, making me forget what I was about to say. I let out a low moan as his hands slowly roamed over my body. Every kiss, every touch set my soul on fire.

"I missed you," Bobby groaned. He lifted his body from mine just long enough to remove his jeans and toss them to the floor. When he leaned back over me, I gently ran my fingers over the bandage that was wrapped around his arm. The reality of what could have happened to him crashed down over me. If that bullet had hit him just a few inches closer to his chest, he wouldn't have even been there with me. My heart ached just thinking about it.

"I'm okay, Court," he whispered, brushing the tears from my cheek.

I brought my hands up to his chest and trailed my fingertips over the defined muscles of his abdomen. My eyes roamed over his body, stopping when our eyes met. His gaze was filled with lust, and it made my body tense with need. I squirmed below him, craving his touch. He put his hands under my knees and pulled me closer to him, pressing his erection against me. He brushed his hard cock against my clit as he asked, "Are you ready for me, baby?"

"Yes," I cried out.

My fingers twisted in the sheets as he brought my knees up to his chest, driving into me with one deep thrust. My head flew back as he rocked back and forth, grinding against me. Each move was slow and deliberate. He was driving me wild with anticipation. I felt his rough, calloused fingers as his hands eased under my shirt and pulled it up to expose my breasts. He bent over me, taking my breast in his hand and latching his mouth onto my nipple. He flicked his tongue back and forth over my hard flesh, sending electric surges throughout my body. I raked my nails down his back as he continued to torment me with his tongue.

His hand slowly moved down my body until it rested between us. He pressed the pad of his thumb against my clit, rubbing in hard circles.

"Fuck!" I cried out, turning my head towards the pillow beside me, hoping that it would muffle my scream.

He smashed his lips against mine as he continued to torture me with his every move. I lifted my hips, shamelessly grinding against him. He groaned loudly against my mouth as he continued his onslaught. I arched my back, pressing my breasts against his chest. A long, anguished moan ripped through my chest as every muscle in my body began to tremble. I jolted beneath him as my orgasm finally hit me, throwing me into a fit of ecstasy. His nose tucked into my neck as he continued to thrust harder and faster inside of me. His chest glistened with sweat as his rhythm continued to increase. Every muscle in his body tensed as his own climax began to take hold. His fingers dug into my hips as he thrust into me one last time. A deep growl filled the room as he finally came inside me.

He lowered his hot body down on top of me, resting his head against my chest. I slowly ran my fingers through his damp hair and listened quietly to the rhythm of his breathing. He didn't move from that spot for several minutes, and I thought he might have fallen asleep. I liked the thought of him sleeping that way, resting between my legs. When he started to move, I wrapped my arms around him, urging him to stay where he was.

"I'm too heavy, baby. You won't be able to get any sleep like this," he said as he looked up at me.

"I don't care. I want you close to me," I told him as I ran my fingers through his hair once more.

He laid his head back against my chest and closed his eyes. He was quiet for a moment before he said, "I like being close to you, too, baby." It was the last thing he said before he finally drifted off to sleep.

I woke up the next morning with Bobby sleeping soundly beside me. At some point in the night, he must have rolled off of me without me realizing it. I carefully eased myself out of bed, trying my best not to wake him. It was close to 7:00 a.m., and I desperately needed a shower and a strong cup of coffee. I tiptoed into the bathroom and quietly shut the door. The hot water eased my aching muscles.

Bobby was still sleeping when I came out of the bathroom, so I put on some clothes and headed to the kitchen. Lily was sitting at the table feeding John Warren when I walked in. I hadn't seen him since the night of the accident, and I had to fight the urge to run over to him. Lily smiled as I walked over to them.

"Look who came to see you, JW!" she said, pointing over in my direction.

I crouched down beside his high chair and said, "Hey

there, little man. It's so good to see you!"

He smiled at me as he crammed another Cheerio into his mouth. I couldn't believe how much he'd grown since the last time I'd seen him. Just another reminder of how much I'd missed over the past couple of months. "You've gotten so big!"

"Isn't it crazy? He's going through a growth spurt or something," Lily said as she ran her fingers over the top of his little head. She turned back to me and said, "Welcome to the nut house."

"I'm sure it's going to be loads of fun," I told her sarcastically.

"It hasn't been that bad really. I've been a little hard to tolerate lately with my out of control hormones and morning sickness. I'm sure everyone is ready to get away from me," she said, smiling.

"How far along are you now?" I asked.

"Almost 12 weeks. We'll get to find out if it's a boy or a girl in a month or so."

"Does John Warren want a brother or a sister?" I asked as I looked over to him. I couldn't help but smile watching him shovel that cereal into his mouth. That boy loved his Cheerios.

"I'm sure he doesn't care either way, but I'm kinda hoping for a girl," Lily said as she ran her hand across her belly. She was barely showing, but she definitely had that pregnancy glow that everyone talked about. She'd always been beautiful, but now happiness seemed to radiate from her.

"What about your folks? Have you told them yet?" I

asked.

"I told my mother…. She isn't exactly thrilled, but I know she'll be fine with it as soon as she meets Goliath," she said as she put more Cheerios in John Warren's bowl.

"He's going to be a great father, Lily. He's been wonderful with John Warren. I'm sure your mother will love him," I told her.

"I think she's still having a hard time getting over the mess with Hailey. She really wanted to blame Maverick for everything that happened, but I think she's finally coming to terms with the truth," Lily explained.

"I can understand that. It had to be hard to find out that your daughter had lied to you for all those months. I can't believe she told her mother that Maverick was after her."

"It was awful. I really felt bad for him. I'm just glad it's all over, and now Goliath and I can move on from all of this," she said with a smile.

Goliath walked in and headed straight over to Lily. I'd almost forgotten how big he really was until he leaned down to give her a kiss on the lips. He turned to me and asked, "How's Bobby making it?"

"He's okay, I guess. He's still sleeping," I told him. "It was pretty late when he got in last night."

"Tell him to find me when he wakes up. I need to talk to him," he said as he poured himself a cup of coffee.

"I'll go see if he's awake. I'll be sure to tell him you need to see him," I told him as I headed back to Bobby's room.

I was expecting him to still be sleeping, but he was already up. I could hear the shower running as I stepped closer to the bathroom. I smiled as a mischievous thought crossed my mind.

CHAPTER 18

Love doesn't make the world go 'round. Love is what
makes the ride worthwhile.

Franklin P. Jones

BOBBY

WHEN I ROLLED over in the bed, I wasn't happy to find that Courtney had already gotten up. I'd had plans for her that morning, but I figured she'd had to get ready for work. I pulled myself out of bed and headed to the bathroom for a shower. I had to get moving if I was going to get her to work on time.

After I turned on the water, I checked my bandage. Mac had said that I needed to try to keep it dry for the first few days. I was already tired of fucking with it. The pain wasn't as intense, but it still throbbed whenever I tried to move it. I decided against taking my pain medicine, hoping a hot shower might ease some of the discomfort.

I'd just finished washing my hair when the shower door slid open. Courtney stood there wearing only a smile on her face. She slowly stepped into the shower, and without saying a word, she dropped down to her knees. My cock twitched as her hands trailed up my legs. Her greedy eyes stared at my growing erection, and her fingers gently moved up and down my thick shaft. I was completely lost the moment her tongue touched the head of my dick. She started slowly, flicking her tongue lightly against the tip before swirling it in her mouth. Her fingers tightened around my cock as she continued to work her hand up and down my dick. Her mouth felt so fucking good wrapped around me. My hands twisted in her damp hair, guiding her. She continued to suck and stroke me as I pushed further into her mouth. Her pace quickened as my cock began to throb. The combination of the hot water from the shower and the soft warmth of her mouth sent me over the edge. A low hiss slid through my clenched jaw as she pulled me deeper into her mouth. Her moan vibrated through her throat as my cock pulsed inside her.

A sly smile crossed her face as I reached down and pulled her up from her knees. "Good morning," she said playfully.

She continued to surprise me. I couldn't imagine what my life would've been like without her in it.

"You're going to be late to work, baby," I told her.

"Not going. I called in so I could spend the day with you," she said as she ran her fingers across my chest. "Now, let's get out so I can change your bandage."

I nodded and followed her out of the shower so we could dry off. Once we were both dressed, Courtney made fast work of removing my bandage. She did her best not to freak out over the grotesque wound, but I could tell that it bothered her. A pained look crossed her face as she applied the antiseptic. I flinched momentarily as the sting of the medicine bore through my arm.

"Does it hurt?" she asked.

"It's not that bad," I told her as I gave her a quick kiss on the lips. I reached for a towel and asked, "What did you want to do today?" I wanted to distract her from my wounded arm. That was something she didn't need to worry about.

"I don't care as long as I get to spend some time with you. Oh, and Goliath wants you to come find him. He said he needed to talk to you," she said with her brows furrowed.

"I'll meet up with him later. I've got a few things to take care of first," I told her as I wrapped my arms around her waist.

She brought her hands up to my face, brushing her fingertips across the bristles of my beard. "Oh, yeah? What exactly do you have to take care of?" she asked, smiling seductively.

"You, baby. Just you." She wrapped her legs around my waist as I lifted her from the floor.

A sexy smile spread across her face as she said, "I like your way of thinking."

I carried her back to my bed and spent the next few hours making good use of her day off. She'd fallen asleep cradled in my arms, and I laid there with her for almost an hour just watching her sleep. I was just about to fall asleep myself when there was a knock on my door. I eased up from the bed, already knowing who was waiting for me on the other side of the door. I was pulling my pants on when he knocked again.

"I'm coming," I muttered as I opened the door. Goliath was standing there with his arms crossed over his chest.

"Fuck, Crack Nut. It's been almost three hours," he snapped.

I shrugged my shoulders. There really wasn't anything for me to say to that. "Let me grab a shirt," I told him. I was actually impressed that he'd waited as long as he had to come find me. Goliath wasn't known for his patience.

I followed him to Bishop's office. He was waiting for us when we walked in.

"About time, brother," Bishop said.

"You talk to Snake?" I asked.

"I did. He's worked out a plan. I wanted to discuss it with both of you before I agreed," Bishop said with concern.

"Let's hear it," Goliath said.

"He wants to use their webcams to draw the Black Diamonds out. He mentioned that you're the one who gave him the idea," he said looking over to me.

"I did," I replied.

"He wants to set up an ambush at the dam near Calvert City. The Davenports have a dock there. He has a friend that's a barge pilot that agreed to let us use his barge to stage a delivery."

"Where do we come in to play?" Goliath asked.

"We'd basically be there as backup," he said.

"You really think that will work?" Goliath asked.

"The minute the Black Diamonds hear that Snake is planning to infringe on their idea, they are gonna lose their shit. They'll be there to make sure it never goes down," I told them both.

"That's what Snake is counting on," Bishop stated.

"When?" Goliath asked.

"He's waiting on me to make that call. He said he wouldn't do anything until I had time to discuss it with the club," he replied.

"Good. You gonna call for a vote?" Goliath asked.

"Yes. We'll meet for church tonight at 7. Let the brothers know that I expect them all to be there," he told Goliath.

Goliath walked out of the office, leaving me alone with Bishop.

"You did good, Crack Nut. We wouldn't be able to do this without you," Bishop told me.

"I'd do anything for my family, Bishop. I just hope this all plays out the way it needs to," I told him.

"We'll just have to make sure it does," he said confidently.

I nodded and headed back to find Courtney. When she wasn't in my room, I went to look for her in the kitchen. She was talking to Lily when I walked in.

"I can go with you. Do you have a list of everything you need?" she asked Lily.

"It's not much. Just some stuff for John Warren. We can ask the guys if they need anything while we're out,"

Lily replied.

"Sounds good to me. I could use a little fresh air," Courtney said with a sigh.

"You aren't going anywhere," I snapped.

CHAPTER 19

COURTNEY

B OBBY SURPRISED ME with his angry tone. It wasn't like him to react so quickly. "We weren't planning to go alone, Bobby. We know the *rules*, but Lily needs to get some things," I told him, placing my hands on my hips. I hated to admit it, but I kind of liked his bossy tone.

"Have you told Goliath?" Bobby asked Lily.

"He's been busy all morning, so I haven't had a chance to talk to him yet," she answered.

"I'll get Levi and Bull to go with us, but make sure you get the okay from Goliath before we go," Bobby told her.

"I'll go find him. Thanks, Bobby," Lily replied as she headed to go look for Goliath.

I walked over to Bobby and placed the palm of my hand on the side of his face. "I like it when you get all protective," I said pressing my body against his.

"Get used to it, baby. I'm not gonna let anything happen to you again," he whispered.

"Good. Shouldn't we see if anybody else needs anything while we're out?" I asked him.

He let out a deep sigh before he said, "Probably, but they are gonna ask for a lot of shit. It's gonna take a while."

"That's fine. It'll be fun to get out of here for a little bit," I told him.

"No, Courtney. This isn't going to be a fun trip. This is just a run for supplies. You are *not* going on one of your shopping escapades," Bobby snapped.

"I know, I know," I told him. "No fun. Just supplies. I get it." I rolled my eyes and followed him down the hall to find out who needed *supplies*. Supplies? Whatever. It was shopping, no matter how you sliced it.

After we asked around, we had a long list of things to get while we were out. Bobby was right. The guys had a lot that they wanted us to get for them, including toilet paper, liquor, cigarettes, and dip. It wasn't going to be a short trip. Apparently, it had been days since anyone had been shopping, and they were low on everything.

We made several stops before heading into the supermarket. We had a pretty extensive list, so we decided to make it faster by dividing it. Bobby agreed to let Bull follow Lily and I over to the baby section, while he and Levi gathered up the groceries.

"Stay with Bull," he told me. "I'll be close."

I nodded and smiled, knowing there was no way he would let me get out of his sight. When we got to the baby section, Lily and I became enthralled with all of the cute clothes they'd just put out on display.

"Look at this one!" I told her as I ran my fingers

across the soft fabric. "I really hope you have a girl. It will be so much fun dressing her up in all of these cute clothes."

"I'll probably go overboard, but I can't wait. There are just too many adorable things!" She picked up a little dress and turned to Bull and said, "Isn't this one precious?"

He didn't answer. He just rolled his eyes and smiled.

"Well, I think it's adorable. Let's buy it," I told her.

"No... not yet. I don't want to jinx anything," Lily said with concern.

"I get that, but you don't have anything to worry about. Everything is going to be fine with you and the baby."

"I know. It's just all this lockdown stuff has me worried about everything. I'll get over it," she confessed.

"It'll all be over soon, Lily," I told her.

"God, I hope so. I'm not much for being cooped up for long periods of time."

"Amen, sister. We need to do something fun when this thing is over. By then, we'll have lots to celebrate."

We continued to look around the baby aisle and occasionally threw things into the cart. "You didn't tell me that Bobby gave you your jacket," Lily told me with her hand on her hip.

"I guess there really hasn't been a good time to tell everyone," I told her.

"I just wanted you to know that I'm happy for you. I'm glad you and Bobby worked everything out."

"I was beginning to have my doubts, but I love him.

I always have," I told her. We'd just about filled the entire cart when I got this weird sensation that someone was watching me. I stopped and looked around, but I didn't notice anything out of the ordinary. There were a few customers doing their own shopping, and a mother was fussing at her son, but nothing unusual. Everyone looked completely normal, so I decided to ignore it. I figured it was just one of my students gawking at me. My kids never seemed to get that I had a life outside of that classroom. I smiled thinking how surprised they were when they saw me out doing everyday things.

I tried to shake off the eerie feeling and looked back over to Lily. She was standing beside Bull as he reached up to the top shelf to grab her a case of diapers. It had been pushed back, and he was having a hard time pulling it down. Lily giggled as she watched him stand on his tiptoes, so he could reach the box. He refused to ask for help. Lily's attention was focused on Bull when a dark figure came up behind her. He stood motionless behind her, and it instantly set me on edge. I tried to get a glimpse of him, but Lily was blocking his face. Chills ran down my spine as he slowly brought his hand up to the side of her head, pointing his fingers at her temple like a gun. Lily was totally unaware of what was happening. I wanted to warn her, but I was frozen in fear. I couldn't comprehend what was going on. It had to be some kind of joke. I couldn't imagine why anyone would do that to Lily. My mouth dropped in horror when the man finally stepped to the side, exposing his face.

The scar. The scar that had haunted my dreams for

weeks was standing right in front of me. My eyes widened in fear as a wicked smile slowly crept across his face. I had no idea what he was going to do. I needed to move, to do something to get Lily's attention. I quickly dropped the jars of baby food. The glass shattered across the floor as I started to scream. No actual words came from my mouth, just blood curdling screams that brought the attention of everyone around us. Within seconds, Bull had dropped the box of diapers and had his gun drawn, ready to take action. He looked for my source of terror, but the man with the grotesque scar was nowhere to be seen.

"It was him!" I shouted. I looked around us trying to find where he might have gone, but he was nowhere to be found.

"Who?" Bull asked frantically. "Who was it?" Several customers gasped when they saw the gun in his hand, but he just ignored them. My heart pounded in my chest, and my thoughts raced through my head. I kept seeing him standing there, smiling like he did in my nightmares.

"It was... him," I stammered. "From the night of the accident. The man with the scar," I pleaded with them, trying to make them understand who I was talking about. "He was standing right behind you. Pointing his fingers at you like this," I said as I showed her what he'd done. A look of horror washed over her as she listened to my words. She shook her head, realizing the man had already gone.

Lily rushed over to me and wrapped her arms around me. "Courtney, he's gone, honey. It's okay," she said, trying to calm me down.

Levi rushed over to us and said, "Bobby had eyes on Courtney the whole time. When he saw what happened he followed him out the door."

"What?! *By himself?*" I screeched.

"Goddamn it!" Bull shouted.

"He didn't want me to leave you. He told me to get y'all back to the clubhouse. *Now*," he demanded.

"I gotta call Bishop first," Bull said as he reached for his phone.

After Bull called Bishop and told him everything that had happened, we had to stay where we were. Bishop didn't want us to leave until Goliath and Renegade got there. He didn't want to risk having anyone cause us problems on the way home. I was a nervous wreck. It didn't take long for them to come rushing into the store. Goliath went straight to Lily and held her close to him as he led her out of the store. Renegade took me by the arm, and we followed them out to the truck.

Bobby was still gone when we made it back to the clubhouse. Pacing around his room, I prayed that he'd come back home safely. I hated feeling so damn helpless. Bobby was putting his life at risk, and there was nothing I could do to stop him. I wanted the nightmare to be over, but I knew the worst was yet to come.

It was hours before Bobby got back to the club-house. He charged into the bedroom, closing the door behind him. He walked over to me and wrapped his arms around my waist and buried his face in my neck. The warmth of his breath soothed me as he held me tight against him. Neither of us spoke. I held him until the tension in his muscles began to relax.

"I was worried out of my mind," I whispered.

"I'm fine. No need for you to worry, baby. This will all be over soon," he told me.

"I'm scared," I confessed.

He didn't respond. He brought his hand to my face and kissed me. It wasn't an answer, but it would do. I trusted Bobby, and I tried to focus on what Maverick had told me a few days ago. *"Sometimes we just have to live on faith, Courtney. Believe in Bobby the way he believes in you."* I did have faith in Bobby, and I had to trust him to take care of everything.

CHAPTER 20

Love has its place, as does hate.

Peace has its place, as does war.

Mercy has its place, as do cruelty and revenge.

Meir Kahane

BOBBY

"THE GUY WITH the scar. What do we know about him?" Goliath asked.

"His name is Shadow. He's the president of the club. You take him down, and his club will fall with him," I told him.

"We need to keep an eye out for him. I don't want him walking away from this," Goliath snapped.

"He won't if I have anything to do with it," I replied.

Bishop nodded. He knew that neither of us would let him get away with what he'd done. "Everything is going as planned. They took the bait," Bishop told us. "They think Snake has set up a meet with a barge company in Calvert City. They'll try to do whatever they can to make sure that doesn't happen."

"Who are you taking with you?" Bull asked.

"Everyone will go except you, Doc, and the prospects. We'll need you here to watch over our families
while we're gone."

Bull nodded, but I could tell by the expression on his
face that he wasn't happy about staying behind. He
wanted to be part of the action, but we needed him there
more. There was no way Bishop would leave his family
unprotected.

"We leave tomorrow at 2:00. Goliath, you, and Renegade load the truck with any weapons we may need.
You know they're well armed. We'll need to be prepared," Bishop told them.

"On it," Renegade replied.

"Bobby, we're going to need some of your two-way
radios for tomorrow. Bring the ones with an earpiece,"
Bishop told me.

"I'll get them," I nodded.

"Get some rest. I need you at your best tomorrow,"
Bishop told us.

We all dispersed and tried to prepare ourselves for
what lay ahead. Sheppard followed Otis to the bar, while
Renegade headed towards the garage. Goliath stayed to
talk with Bishop, while I went to find Courtney.

Taylor saw me in the hall and said Courtney was
waiting for me in my room. When I walked in, she was
propped up on my bed with several movies sitting in
front of her. She also had enough junk food for ten
people spread across the foot of the bed. She smiled at
me and said, "Thought you might wanna get your mind
off things for a bit."

Fuck. I loved how she always knew what I needed, even when I didn't. I sat down on the bed beside her and said, "I've got a better way to take my mind off things."

"Well, duh. We'll do that later," she said with a laugh and threw a pillow at me. "Now, pick a movie." It was the perfect way to spend the night. Just being with her took my mind off of everything. She was everything I'd ever wanted and more.

WE WERE ABOUT to walk right into a war filled with chaos and destruction. Tension was running so high among the brothers as we crossed into Kentucky that no one bothered talking. We were lost in our own thoughts. I noticed Sheppard seemed a little more on edge than usual. He wasn't the type to let things get to him, but I could tell that something was bothering him. I was just ready to get things taken care of, so we could get back to the way things used to be.

As soon as we pulled into the cargo area, Snake started barking orders at his men. He had them scattered throughout the area, leaving no chance for the Black Diamonds to get away. Bishop didn't want any witnesses, so he had the barge pilot release his crew for the day. The pilot seemed nervous, but Bishop talked to him and assured him that everything would go as planned.

Bishop pulled Snake to the side to discuss the expectations for the day. He gave Snake one of the earpieces I'd given him, so that they would be able to communicate back and forth. Once they finished talking, Bishop walked back over to us and instructed each of us where to go. Sheppard shook his head when Bishop told him to go to one of the rooftops.

"That's too far. I need a better angle. We have to keep you out of the line of fire. I'll take cover on the barge," he protested.

"That's not necessary," Bishop barked.

"The hell it isn't. I'm not taking any chances," he retorted as Goliath handed him his weapon. "I've got your back, brother," he said as he walked towards the boat ramp.

"Be careful, Shep," Bishop warned.

"Always," he shouted as he walked away.

I didn't like him being away from the group, but I trusted Sheppard. He'd been through much worse and come out on the other side. No one seemed surprised by his actions as we each took an earpiece and headed to our assigned location. Bishop asked me to monitor all the security cameras. They monitored everything coming in and out of the area, so I would have no problem knowing when our guests arrived.

It was getting closer to 2:00, so Snake and Bones began loading the barge with empty crates. They didn't want the Black Diamonds to have any doubts about it being an actual shipment. They continued to go back and forth from the truck to the barge.

Goliath looked over to me and shook his head. We both were beginning to think that the Black Diamonds weren't going to show. We'd seen them preparing to come on their surveillance video, but maybe it was just a ploy.

Renegade stepped out from behind the shop and had started to walk over to Bishop when I noticed two men walking behind one of the larger buildings. I called over the radio for him to return to his previous location, but he ignored me. Three more men appeared on the screen just as Renegade reached Bishop. I radioed over to Bishop to let him know that they were there. I watched as six more men made their way towards the barge. I gave my count to Bishop, and he let Snake know they were coming.

Snake and Bones carried on like nothing was happening until Razor, the Black Diamond's VP, approached them with two other men at his side. I was too far away to hear what they were saying, but it was obvious that they were having a heated argument. I kept my eye on the surveillance video and watched as twelve additional men approached the area. It was more than we'd expected, but we were prepared for that.

After several words were exchanged between Razor and Snake, Snake raised his gun and shot him in the head. The two men beside him quickly fell to the ground. I radioed over to Bishop, warning him that the other men were approaching. My pulse raced as gunfire exploded around us. The battle had begun.

CHAPTER 21

COURTNEY

WAITING WAS HELL. Waiting for news alone was unbearable, so we gathered around the bar and waited together. We needed something to take our minds off of things, so Tessa started a debate among the girls.

"No way, Bishop is way more pushy than Goliath," Tessa said with a laugh. "When he tells you to jump, he expects you to ask how high."

"He's older and more authoritative. That doesn't make him pushy," Lily explained.

"Goliath is a man that knows what he wants. He doesn't give a shit about what anyone else thinks," Taylor told us. "I think it's kinda hot."

"Renegade is no pussycat either, my dear," Lily told her, giggling. "I've heard him give you an order or two."

"That's the understatement of the century," Taylor said as she rolled her eyes. "That man is determined to have it his way."

"What about Bobby?" Lily asked. "He doesn't seem to be all that bossy."

"He is when it counts," I said wiggling my eyebrows.

"I love that about him."

"I'm so glad you two worked it out," Tessa started. "You had me worried there for a little while."

"I guess it was the path I had to take. I needed that time to sort through everything, and in the end, I think we're better for it." I wanted to change the subject so I asked, "So, who's got the shortest temper?"

They each said their better half at the same time. We all laughed, and I said, "I'm going with Goliath, just because I wouldn't ever want to piss that man off. He's huge and has all those bulging muscles. Let's face it, he's kinda scary when he's mad."

"He's only scary when he needs to be," Lily said defensively. "But, you're right. He's not the kind of man you want to piss off."

We talked for several hours and then fell silent. It was well after two o'clock. We'd all heard them discussing the times today when they didn't think we were listening. We knew when the trouble would start.

"Do you think they will call us when it's over?" I asked.

"Bishop will text me when they're heading back," Tessa answered. "It shouldn't be much longer."

"What if something went wrong?" I asked. "What if one of them is hurt?"

"We can't think that way, Court. We just can't," Tessa said with concern.

"It's just so damn hard. I love Bobby so much. I don't think I could handle it if something ever happened to him," I cried.

Tessa placed her hand on my shoulder and said, "We all feel that way, honey. We have to remember that they are out there trying to protect us. They'll do anything to keep their family safe."

"How do you do that?" I asked.

"What?" Tessa asked.

"You always have these grand words of wisdom when someone is having doubts. Do you think this stuff up ahead of time, or does it just come to you?" I asked, laughing.

"Shut up, Courtney. Stop giving me a hard time," Tessa said as she nudged me with her shoulder.

"I didn't say it was a bad thing. You are a great First Lady," I told her nudging her back. I meant what I said. Tessa did a great job of keeping things together around there. Bishop knew what he was doing when he chose her. They truly did make the perfect couple.

"I have some news. I shouldn't be telling you this, since I haven't even told Bishop, but..." Tessa started.

"A secret?" I asked. "I love secrets. Come on... spill it. We won't tell. It will go in the vault! Promise!" I said, urging her on.

"I really shouldn't. I feel awful even thinking about telling you all this," Tessa said as she shook her head. "This isn't the time to even talk about it."

"It will take our minds off of things for a bit. We won't say anything," Lily said with a smile. "Like Courtney said, we'll put it in the vault."

"Okay.... Well, I don't know anything for sure, but I'm usually very regular and whatnot," Tessa said and then hesitated.

I nudged her and asked, "And?"

"It's just… it's just that I'm a little late," she said as her face blushed with embarrassment.

"You're *pregnant*?" Lily asked.

"I don't know for sure. I haven't even taken a pregnancy test. We've been on this stupid lockdown, so I haven't been able to buy one without everybody knowing."

"I have one in my room!" Lily said. "Goliath made me buy three different kinds at Christmas. I only used the first one. The others are in my bag."

"*Tess*! You have to take the test!" I pleaded.

"I can't do that without Bishop. He would never let me hear the end of it," Tessa told us.

"I have two. Take one with us, and save the other one for him," Lily said with a wicked grin.

"I like her way of thinking! Come on, Tessa. Let's go find out if you're knocked up," I told her, laughing.

"Okay, but you all have to promise to keep it in the vault. Either way… no one says a word," she demanded. She shook her head and said, "I can't believe I'm doing this."

We all waited as Lily went to her room to get the pregnancy tests. She came back with an excited expression on her face. "We could be pregnant together! I would so love that."

"Don't get ahead of yourself. It's probably nothing. The stress has just made me late or something," Tessa said as she took the test in her hand. "I'll be right back."

She ran into the restroom waving the box above her head. "Hurry!" I shouted.

The room fell silent when she walked back into the room. Her face was void of expression, so we didn't know what to think.

"Well?" I asked.

A huge smile spread across her face as she said, "I'm pregnant!"

We all stood up and raced over to her, hugging her excitedly. "I'm so happy for you!" I told her.

"How am I going to raise four children?" she asked. "I'm just now getting a handle on having three!"

"You are a wonderful mother, Tessa. You're a natural. Don't worry about that," Lily told her.

"What will Bishop think?" Tessa asked. "We've never even talked about having another child."

"You're about to make him the happiest man on the planet. Don't you worry one minute about what Bishop is going to think. He loves you. I have no doubt in my mind that he is going to be thrilled to death over this baby," I told her.

"I can't believe I'm going to have a baby," Tessa said.

"I know the feeling," Lily told her. "I don't think that feeling ever goes away."

"I can't wait to see the expression on his face when I tell him he's going to be a father," Tessa told us.

"How much longer is this going to take? It's been hours," Taylor asked, bringing us back to reality. "Shouldn't they have called by now?"

Gloom filled the room as we all looked over at the clock. We had no idea how long they would be, and we were all beginning to worry. I had to believe that they would call us soon.

CHAPTER 22

The best weapon against an enemy is another enemy.
Friedrich Nietzsche

BOBBY

W E WERE SURROUNDED by gunfire as I watched the additional men approach the area. Snake's men continued to take them out, one by one. There was still no sign of Shadow. We all knew that it wouldn't be over until Shadow was dead. When bullets started heading in our direction, Goliath began to fire back. Bishop joined him, but neither of them were able to stop the man that was shooting in their direction. I had a better angle, so without hesitation, I pulled out my weapon and shot him. When he fell to the ground, Bishop looked over in my direction and nodded in approval.

When I looked back at the screen, I saw a black Tahoe slowly pulling into the lot. I radioed over to Bishop to let him know that it was heading in our direction. The tinted windows slowly came down, unveiling the barrel of a semi-automatic rifle. Gunfire rained from the windows, as a man slipped out the back door. The man slowly made his way over to the side of the building, and when he stopped, I finally recognized him. Shadow.

"He's here," I told Goliath over the two-way radio.

"Where?" he asked.

"He's coming around the south side of the main warehouse. He's getting closer. Just a few more steps," I told him.

"I got it," Goliath told me.

Goliath reached for his long distance rifle with a mounted scope. He propped the gun on his shoulder, and patiently waited for Shadow to come into sight.

I watched Shadow inch closer to Snake, totally unaware that we were watching him. His sole focus was on getting to Snake. He was oblivious to the fact that death waited for him just around the corner. With his gun in his hand, he crept along the backside of the building. He seemed totally unfazed as he stepped over his fallen brothers that were scattered along the ground.

When Shadow took the first step out into the open, Goliath didn't hesitate taking his shot. A look of total surprise crossed his face as the bullet pierced through his head. His limp body fell helpless to the ground. I looked over to Goliath. The gun remained in its previous position as Goliath glared at the dead man's body. With an angry grimace, he looked back into the scope and shot him three more times.

The remaining Black Diamond members became frantic when they saw their president fall dead, shooting at anything in sight. When the gunfire became directed towards Bishop, Sheppard revealed himself. He fired off several rounds, killing three of the men shooting in our direction. At that moment, all attention was drawn to Sheppard. He ducked down, trying to escape the bullets that were then directed at him, but he wasn't fast enough. Two bullets slammed into his chest with such force that it knocked him off the barge and into the rapidly moving waters of the lake. We all watched helplessly as his body was taken by the fast moving current.

"Goddamn it!" Bishop shouted. He jumped up and ran to the edge of the water. Goliath and Renegade followed quickly behind him, ignoring the gunfire that surrounded them.

"Watch out, Bishop," Goliath shouted as he tackled him to the ground, covering him with his own body. Gunfire continued to erupt around them. I tried to kill the shooter myself, but he was out of my range.

"I've got to get to him," Bishop shouted as he shook Goliath off of him. He made his way over to the water's edge and searched for any sign of Sheppard. Silence surrounded us as the final two men were killed, leaving no Black Diamond left alive.

Bishop pulled off his leather jacket and tossed it to the ground. Goliath grabbed him by the arm and said, "Don't! You'll never get to him like that. We need to find a boat."

"There's no time!" Bishop shouted.

"You'll drown before you ever even reach him, brother! You gotta know that," Goliath pleaded with him.

Renegade raced over to the barge pilot and asked him for help. He gave him the keys to his old johnboat but warned him against trying to find Sheppard.

"There's not much you're going to be able to do. We're right by the spillway, and the dam is running. The current is too strong here," he told us. "Even if the gunshots didn't kill him, the water will. There's no way he'll survive that."

"I don't give a fuck," Goliath said as he took the keys from Renegade. "We gotta try."

We spent four hours searching for Sheppard but never found any trace of him.

We considered calling for help, but it was a double-edged sword. The police might have been able to find him, but there was no way that we could explain the mayhem that surrounded us. We had to give up the search. It was dark, and we knew there was little chance that we'd ever find him alive. We'd lost our brother. There was nothing more we could do for him.

CHAPTER 23

COURTNEY

————⧫⧫⧫————

"WHY HAVEN'T WE heard from them yet?" I asked Tessa.

"I'm not sure. Bishop always calls me," she said with concern. We were all expecting them to let us know something, and since they hadn't tried calling, we knew that something must have been wrong.

"Maybe Bull has heard something," Taylor said. "I'll go see if he knows anything."

"Doubt he will tell us anything, but it's worth a try," Tessa told her. We all followed her to the bar in search of Bull.

He was talking with Levi when we walked into the room.

"It can't be good. They should've been back hours ago," Bull mumbled to Levi.

"Should we go see if we can find them?" Levi asked.

"We can't leave the clubhouse unprotected. It's too big of a risk. We may need to go to the lakehouse at Big Sandy. If something went wrong, the Black Diamonds will come here looking for us," Bull told him.

"We're not leaving until we hear from Bishop," Tessa said firmly. "He would find a way to let us know if we were in danger."

Bull looked surprised to see us standing there, but he didn't hesitate when he said, "You'll go where you're told, when you're told. It's my job to make sure you're safe, and that's exactly what I plan to do."

"I'm not going anywhere, Bull. I will be standing right here when Bishop walks through that door," she demanded.

"We'll give it another hour, but if we don't hear from them, we *will* make the move," Bull told her. He looked over to Levi and said, "Tell Conner that we are on high alert. If he sees anything suspicious, I want to know about it. You monitor the surveillance feed."

"You got it, brother," Levi told him as he left the bar.

"I want everyone together. Get the kids and go to the family room. Wait there," he ordered.

"Do you really think that's necessary?" I asked. "The kids are watching a movie in my room."

"Now," he ordered. He stood up and walked out of the room without saying another word.

"This is making me crazy," Lily said as tears streamed down her face. "I'm texting Goliath. I have to know if he's okay."

"Don't. They told us not to contact them. We don't want to draw any attention to them if they're in a bad situation," Tessa told her. "Let's get the kids and do like Bull asked. Courtney, bring one of your games for the kids. We'll need something to entertain them while we wait."

Yep. Tessa made a great First Lady. She always knew the right thing to do, even when everything was going to hell in a handbasket.

The kids didn't mind moving into the family room. I'd actually never been in that room before, and I was surprised by how much it looked like a regular living room. It had a large L-shaped leather sofa and several recliners, and widescreen TV's mounted on the wall. There were several cool paintings of motorcycles spanning the back wall. The kids scrambled around to find their spots as Myles grabbed the remote, turning on their favorite cartoons.

"I'm hungry," Drake whined. "Can we order a pizza or something?"

"Maybe in a little while. We just need to hang out in here for a little bit," Tessa told him.

"Is something bad going on?" he asked. "We've never been allowed in here before."

"Everything is fine, honey. Just wanted to have us all together when the guys got back," she told him as she placed her hand on his shoulder.

"I know when you aren't telling me the truth, Mom. You can tell me what's really going on," he told her. Izzie looked over to her with worry in her eyes. She hadn't even thought about something being wrong until Drake brought it up.

"It's *fine*, Drake," she told him firmly.

"Whatever. Just give me a heads up if the bad guys

are coming to get us. I want to be prepared," he told her as he rolled his eyes.

"Drake!" Tessa fussed. "That's enough."

He gave her a frustrated look as he reached in his pocket for his iPod. He put on his headphones and stared at the wall, trying to tune us out.

"Momma, is Bishop okay?" Izzie asked.

A look of anguish washed over Tessa as she looked over to her daughter. She placed the palm of her hand on Izzie's face and said, "Yes, baby. He's fine. He'll be home soon."

"I hope so. I miss him," Izzie told her.

I felt the tears well up in my eyes as I watched them together. I was overcome with emotion. I fought back the tears as I thought about one of us losing the men we loved so much. It was almost too much to bear.

CHAPTER 24

May the road rise up to meet you, may the wind be
ever at your back. May the sun shine warm upon your
face and the rain fall softly on your fields. And until
we meet again, may God hold you in the hollow of
his hand.

~*Irish Blessing*

BOBBY

W E ALL STOOD on the dock, staring at the water,
watching as the current drifted by our feet like
nothing had ever happened. It was hard to believe that
something that looked so beautiful could be so deadly.
I'd always loved the lake, but now it repulsed me just to
look at it. I hated it for taking my brother away from us.
I couldn't stand the thought of leaving without Sheppard. It just didn't seem right.

"There has to be something else we can do," I told
them.

"He's gone, brother. There's nothing left for us to do
right now," Bishop told me.

"I don't think I can live with that," I told him.

"We have to," Bishop said. "We don't have a choice."

I nodded, but the tightness in my chest made it difficult to breathe. I walked over to Renegade and helped him finish loading the truck. The suffocating feeling of death surrounded us as Snake's men dragged all of the dead bodies into one of the older warehouses. They planned to torch the building as soon as we had the lot cleared. Snake covered the bloodstained concrete with diesel fuel and set it on fire. We were immediately bombarded with the stench of blood and gasoline.

"It's getting late," Goliath told us. "We need to get back."

"Have you called Bull?" I asked Bishop.

"Goddamn it! I should've called hours ago. I'm sure Tessa is freaking out," he said as he reached for his phone. We all waited as he made the call. When he was finished, he walked over to Snake.

"I'm sorry about your loss, brother," Snake told him.

"I appreciate that. Didn't plan on things turning out like this, but I'm glad this shit is over. The Black Diamonds are done, and we can move on."

"You know where to reach me," Snake told him.

"I do," Bishop replied as he extended his hand out to Snake. They shook hands, ending all ties we had to the Red Dragons.

Anger surged through Goliath as he got in the truck. He rubbed his hands down his face and said, "Why couldn't that motherfucker just do what he was told to do? Why did he always have to be the goddamn hero?"

"He was there when we needed him, Goliath. There's no other place he'd rather be," Bishop told him.

"This is fucking insane," Goliath shouted as he slammed his hands against the steering wheel. "We should've made him go to the roof. I should've been the one on that barge."

"It played out the way it needed to play out, Goliath. You can't second guess every move we made," Renegade told him. "Sheppard knew what he was getting into. I wouldn't have expected him to do anything different than what he did."

"I'm not going to stop looking for him," I told them. "I'll find him. Dead or alive. I will find him."

The truck fell silent. They knew I wouldn't give up until I found something that led us to him. Someone would find him, and I'd be there waiting when they did.

CHAPTER 25

COURTNEY

I T'D BEEN ALMOST two weeks since the night we'd lost Sheppard. No one had been able to get past it. It was the not knowing that made it so much more difficult. Bobby wanted to believe that he was still alive. He truly thought there was still a chance that he'd survived. He was consumed with the need to find him; it was the only thing that kept him from completely giving in to his grief. He refused to listen to Goliath and Bishop when they wanted to plan a memorial service for him. He wouldn't accept that Sheppard was dead until they recovered his body. A part of me knew that it was just the guilt talking. They all felt relentless guilt for leaving their brother behind, but they didn't have a choice. I knew they had done everything they could to save him. Realistically, I knew there was little chance that Sheppard had survived. Even without the bullet wounds, he wouldn't have been able to live in that unforgiving river. Nothing could've survived in that current at that time of year.

Bobby and I were stuck in a cyclone of emotion. A

brief moment of happiness would be followed by the crushing grief of losing Sheppard. The sadness around us just kept pulling us into a dark, gloomy place that I desperately needed out of. I had to think of something that would help ease the pain for Bobby, but I was at a loss. I had no idea what to do.

"I need an idea," I told Tessa. We were both back at work and had decided to have lunch together.

"What kind of idea?" she asked.

"I don't know. Some kind of distraction. I need to take Bobby's mind off of things for a while. He's having a hard time getting past losing Sheppard."

"They all are. It's just going to take time. Sheppard was special to them, and they feel like they failed him. We both know they did everything they could, but they will never think it was enough," she explained.

"What can I do?" I asked.

"Just listen to him. Give him the time he needs to find his way through this," Tessa told me.

"You're right. I'll stop trying to fix it. I just wanted to do something to help him," I told her.

"You know, we have Spring Break coming up in a couple of weeks. Why don't you take that trip he planned for you at Christmas? It might be good to get away from here for a while."

"That's an awesome idea! Do you think he'd go for it?" I asked.

"Never know unless you try. Besides, I think it would be good for both of you."

I left there feeling better about things. I needed

something to look forward to. It took a couple of days to get everything together, and I was nervous about bringing it up to Bobby. I wasn't sure how he'd feel about leaving, so I waited until we were getting ready for bed and slipped on his favorite t-shirt and my black lace panties. His eyes roamed over my body appraisingly as he walked into the bedroom. He peeled off his t-shirt and tossed it to the floor, never taking his eyes off me.

"Umm... I ... I have an idea that I want to run by you," I stammered.

He looked over to me with a lopsided grin spread across his face. "Uh, okay. What kind of idea?" he asked as he slowly began to unbuckle his belt.

"Um, well... I thought we could take a little trip over Spring Break. Maybe we could...."

"You mean the trip you've been planning for the last few days?" he asked with a shit-eating grin as he stalked over to me.

"Bobby! Stop looking through the history on my computer! That is an *invasion* of my *privacy*!" I screeched, poking him in the shoulder.

"I didn't have to search your history, babe. It was still up when I logged on. You never closed the page. Besides, I don't have to use a computer to know when you're up to something," he said mischievously as he began to lower his jeans.

"Is that so?" I demanded, putting my hands on my hips.

He stepped closer to me, pressing his body against mine. "That's right, baby. You can't hide anything from me," he said as he leaned down and slowly began nipping at my neck, sending chills down my body.

"And how is that, Bobby? How do you *know* when I'm trying to keep something from you?" I asked flippantly.

"It's written all over your face. Your smile lights up a room when you're happy," he said as his hands traveled across my waist. "You're oddly quiet when you're upset about something, and you won't look me in the eye when you're trying to keep something from me." He put his hands under my ass and lifted me, forcing my legs to wrap around his waist.

"Oh, *really*?" I whispered in his ear.

"You haven't been able to look me in the eye for days, babe. I thought you'd never get around to telling me what you'd planned."

"I wanted it to be a surprise," I told him.

"Consider me surprised," he said as he dropped me to the bed and rested between my legs.

"So can we go?" I asked. "I know you need to do what you can for the club and Sheppard, but Bobby... you and me, we need this."

"We'll go, but I need to see your parents before we leave," he told me as he reached for the hem of my shirt and lifted it over my head.

"My parents? Why do you need to see them? Oh, please lord, don't tell me you want to ask them to go with us," I pleaded as he trailed kisses up my stomach to my breasts. "Because they will. I promise—they will come."

"No, Court. I'm not going to ask them to go with us.

I just need to talk to them. Clear the air a little bit," he told me as he kissed my neck.

I pushed at his shoulder, forcing him to stopping kissing me so I could say, "Why do you want to do that? You know they aren't exactly thrilled about us being back together."

"That's why I want to *clear... the ...air*," he said sarcastically.

"And how are you going to *clear the air*?" I gasped as his fingertips brushed along my breasts.

"Just leave that to me. Ask them over to your place for dinner on Friday night, and I'll handle the rest," he replied as he bent over me.

The bristles of his beard brushed against my cheek as he whispered, "Now... let me tell you what else I'm going to handle." The heat of his breath sent tremors of pleasure throughout me as he said, "I'm going to make you shiver with anticipation as I devour you with my mouth, and I'm going to tease you with my hard cock until you beg for more. Then, I'm going to listen to you become breathless as I drive deep inside you, feeling your pussy tighten around me. I'm going to fuck you slow and hard until your body trembles beneath me, and I'm not going to stop until you come apart around my cock. And I'm going to enjoy every second of watching you lose control."

I couldn't tear my eyes from him as he slowly hooked his thumbs in my panties and slid them down my thighs. He grinned up at me devilishly and said, "Now... lay back and hush."

CHAPTER 26

Love is when the other person's happiness is more important than your own.

H. Jackson Brown, Jr.

BOBBY

———◆◉◉◉◆———

I DON'T KNOW where Courtney got the idea that she wanted to learn to snowboard, but it had to be one of the worst ideas she'd ever had. We spent the entire day out on that mountain, and she couldn't get the hang of it. I had to give her credit, though. She was determined; she just didn't have the coordination for it. I tried my best not to laugh when she fell, but *damn*. That shit was funny. With snow all over her clothes and face, she'd get right back up and try again. She took it all in stride, but finally gave up when she took a nasty fall on her rear. Her ass was going to be black and blue for days.

She took a hot bath, and we spent the rest of the afternoon in the room. I tried everything I could to make her forget about the disaster of the morning, but I could tell it was still bugging her.

"Let's get out of this room and go do something," I

suggested.

"I'd say we just did plenty, don't ya think?" she said with a smile. She was referring to the hours I'd just spent exploring every inch of her beautiful body, but I had big plans for her that night. Hopefully, it would be the surprise of her life.

"We did. Now, we need to go grab dinner, and maybe go see one of those movies you've been talking about," I told her.

"*The Woman in Black*? Can we go see it? The first one was so good!" she said excitedly.

"Yeah, we can go see the lady in black, but we have to get dinner first. I'm starving," I told her.

"Deal," she said as she got up and headed for the shower.

After a quick dinner, we headed over to the local movie theatre. While Courtney grabbed us some snacks, I thought back to the conversation I'd had with her father a few days ago. It had gone better than I'd expected it to. To say the least, he wasn't my biggest fan, but he seemed to respect the fact that I'd come to him. It was important to me that both of her parents knew that I wanted the best for her, and I was willing to do whatever it took to make her happy. I told her dad my plans for our future together, and after a few fatherly threats, he consented. He was a good man, and I was relieved that we were able to come to an understanding.

Courtney walked back over to me with her hands full with popcorn and drinks, and we headed into the theatre. My girl loved her snacks when she watched a movie. She was offering me some popcorn when the lights started to go dim. It took her a few seconds to notice that the regular previews weren't showing.

A confused look crossed her face as the first few pictures of us scrolled across the screen. She looked over to me with a questioning look, and I pointed to the screen, encouraging her to watch the movie. Pictures of her with the girls, the kids in her classroom, and even some of us at the carnival where we first met continuously shifted across the screen. Tears trickled down her cheeks as she watched the different pictures of us together, displaying all the special moments of our life we'd shared so far. She reached over and took my hand in hers, never taking her eyes off of the screen. I'd wanted to find the perfect way to show her how much she meant to me. I'd spent days putting that movie together, trying to find the perfect pictures. I'd even stolen some of her favorites from her phone. Just seeing the expression on her face made it worth the hell I'd get about that later.

"When did you do all of this? I love it," she whispered.

I didn't respond. I wanted her full attention on the screen in front of her. She sat motionless as I eased myself out of my seat. I kept her hand in mine, as I reached into my pocket. I watched her jaw drop as she read the words that came up on the screen. With tears in her eyes, she looked at me and gasped loudly when she noticed that I was down on one knee.

"You gonna answer the question, babe?" I asked her

with a smile.

She hesitated for a second, letting the shock of what was happening wear off. "Yes! Yes, I'll marry you!" she screeched as I slipped the ring on her finger. Her arms wrapped around my neck, hugging me tightly.

"That had to be the sweetest thing anyone has ever done for me," she whispered. "I love you so much."

"I love you, too, Courtney. More than you will ever know," I told her as I pressed my lips against hers.

She pulled away from our embrace just long enough to hold out her hand, looking at the engagement ring I'd given her. "It's so beautiful, Bobby. I absolutely love it!"

"Tessa helped me pick it out," I confessed. "I wanted to make sure you'd like it."

"It's perfect," she answered, wiping the tears from her face.

"I want you to move in with me when we get back home," I told her. "My place is bigger, and it's closer to your work. I don't want to wait a minute longer to start our life together."

"Only if I can redecorate," she laughed. "I'm not really into the whole bachelor pad thing you've got going," she said playfully.

"I can handle that. Just no pink. I hate pink," I told her. I honestly didn't care what she did to that place as long as she was there with me. I was sick of going back and forth between her place and mine, and I was looking forward to having her there all the time.

"Can we go home early?" she asked.

"For you, anything," I replied as she pressed her lips against mine.

ANA

"YOU HAVE TO help me," I pleaded.

"What exactly do you want me to do here, Ana?" my father asked.

"I don't know, but we have to do something! He's going to die if we just leave him here," I told him.

"That's exactly what we need to do. Someone wanted this guy dead. Bad enough to shoot him twice and toss him into the lake. He had to be in some kind of trouble, and the last thing we need around here is more trouble."

I knew he was right, but I just couldn't leave him there like that. There was something about the look on his face that grabbed me. I couldn't explain it. I just had to help him. I had to. I couldn't stand the thought of leaving him there to die.

"Please, Daddy. Just help me get him inside. I'll take care of the rest," I told him.

He walked over to the shed and grabbed my old wheelbarrow. He shook his head as he walked back over to me, "It'll be hard to get him up the hill; he's heavy. He'll probably die anyway. I don't know what you're thinking."

"Thanks, Daddy," I told him, bending down to grab the stranger's feet. My dad reached under his shoulders, and we carefully lifted him up into the wheelbarrow. His head tossed from side to side as we pushed him up the path that led to the house. It was the same trail I took every morning when I went on one of my walks. It was the best way I knew to clear my head of all of the chaos that surrounded me. I set out that morning thinking that it might actually be a good day. I hadn't had any strange calls, and I hadn't felt like anyone was watching me for the first time in weeks. I was feeling pretty good about things until I'd stumbled across the man laying limp on the edge of the water. I'd pulled his body out of the lake, and my heart hurt when I'd noticed his blood covered clothes. I'd immediately called my father, knowing I'd never be able to help him alone.

"Where do you want me to put him?" he asked.

"Let's try to get him to the guest room. I'll need your help getting these wet clothes off of him," I told him.

"I think you've got more to worry about than a few wet clothes. This guy needs a hospital," he told me.

"You know I can't take him there," I replied. "Let me see what I can do to help him first. If there's nothing I can do, we'll think of something else." I'd dedicated the last five years of my life to working at our local hospital, but I couldn't even think of calling them for help. It was just too risky.

"I'll work on the clothes, and you go get your medical bag. Make a list of things you might need from town, and I'll go get it."

"Thanks. I really appreciate this," I told him.

"Just be careful, honey. We don't know anything about this guy," he warned.

"I will. Just hurry. We don't have much time," I told him as I headed to my room, preparing myself for what lay ahead.

THE END

Sheppard's story coming soon!

UPDATES

If you want to keep track of my book releases, you can check out my Facebook pages:
www.facebook.com/L.Wilderbooks
www.facebook.com/AuthorLeslieWilder?ref=hl

I am also on Twitter: @wilder_leslie

and Instagram: @Lwilderbooks

ACKNOWLEDGEMENTS

First, I want to thank all you the people that have contacted me over the past few months with your encouraging words. It has meant more to me than you will ever know. It thrills me to no end when I hear that someone enjoyed one of my books. I know I left some of you unhappy with me at the end of Ignite, but it was the way the story played out in my mind. It was up to Bobby to wrap everything up. This is a shorter book, but there is plenty more to come in Sheppard's book. Yes, he will be next, and he will likely be the end of the Devil Chasers' series. I plan to start a completely new series with Maverick and his club this summer.

There are so many people that have helped me along the way, and I want to thank you all. My beta readers and Wilder's Women have been amazing. You continue to encourage me and push me to do my best. I couldn't make it without you.

Marci Ponce takes Beta reading to a whole new level. Your dedication to this book has blown me away. I don't know how to thank you for all of your input. It's meant more to me than you will ever know.

Ana Rosso, my young grasshopper, thank you for always being there to encourage me with your kind words. You make me smile!

I have to give a special thank you to Jordan Marie. She continues to help me with each book, and I am in complete awe of her. She's an amazing blogger and author. If you haven't checked out Not Another Damn Blog Blog, you are missing out. It is amazing. They have great book reviews and tons of giveaways.

www.facebook.com/NotADamnBlog

She is also the author of *Breaking Dragon*. It's an awesome book! Check out her author page:

www.facebook.com/JordanMarieAuthor

My editor, Brooke Asher is incredible. She is patient and understanding, and I couldn't make it without her. She knows that I am neurotic, so she just ignores my insanity. Thank you, girl. I couldn't survive it without you. If you are interested in having her edit your book, you can reach her at brooke.asher.editing@gmail.com. She is easy to work with and very thorough. Contact her about pricing and any other information. You can also find her on Facebook:

www.facebook.com/profile.php?id=100008407952883

My Beta Readers are the best. Sherri Crowder, Patricia Blevins, Savanna Rose, Erin Osborn, Keeanna Porter, Sue Banner, Jenny, Shelley, and Jess Peterson you all mean the world to me. Another special thanks to Jess Peterson for making teasers for all of my books. She is amazing. Thank you so much for reading my books and encouraging me daily. I am blessed to have you in my life.

A final thank you to Jane Mortensen for all the wonderful things you have done to help me along the way. I love your teasers and trailers you've made for my books. It means so much! Be sure to check out her book called Missing Link. It's awesome! The links to my trailers:

Consumed
http://youtu.be/xrD_NtDggLc

Ignite
http://youtu.be/0-rf4R5h3a8

Made in the USA
San Bernardino, CA
15 February 2016